A
Peep Behind
The Scenes

Other children's classics revised
and updated by Christopher Wright:

Christiana's Journey by John Bunyan
Young Christian's Pilgrimage by John Bunyan
Target Earth! by John Bunyan
Christie's Old Organ by Mrs. O.F. Walton
The Rocky Island and Other Stories by Margaret Gatty and
    Samuel Wilberforce

A PEEP BEHIND THE SCENES
Copyright © 1982 this revised edition by Christopher Wright
All rights reserved
Printed in the United States of America
Library of Congress Catalog Card Number: 82-73063
International Standard Book Number: 0-88270-538-5
Bridge Publishing, Inc., South Plainfield, New Jersey 07080

Introduction

In its original form, this was a very, very sad story. It is still sad, but it now has a happy ending. I have been unable to make the story itself not be sad because that would have changed it too much. But I *have* peeled away a lot of the sadness, and found a beautiful story underneath!

This is quite a long book, but an interesting one. I wouldn't be surprised if you read it again quite soon after finishing it the first time!

—Christopher Wright

A PEEP BEHIND THE SCENES

Contents

CHAPTER 1

Rosalie

AIN, rain, rain! All through Sunday it fell on the fair-field. By late afternoon it was heavier than ever. The puddles grew larger and the mud became thicker.

On Saturday evening the Fair had been brilliantly lit with rows of naphtha-lights. The grand shows had been illuminated with flaming crosses, stars, anchors, and all manner of devices to attract the crowds.

But there were no lights now. There was nothing to cast a halo round the dirty, weather-stained tents and caravans.

Yet, in spite of this, and in spite of the rain, a crowd of Sunday strollers lingered about the fair, looking with great interest at the half-covered roundabouts, peeping curiously into the deserted sideshows, and making many schemes for the next day when the fair was once more to be in its glory.

Rosalie

Inside the caravans the show-people were crouching over their fires and grumbling at the weather, murmuring at having to pay so much for the ground on which their shows were erected, at a time when they would be likely to make so little profit!

An old man, with a good-tempered face, was making his way across the sea of mud which divided the shows from each other. He was evidently no sightseer in the fair. He had come into it that Sunday afternoon for a definite purpose, and he did not intend to leave until it was accomplished. After going around the largest patch of mud, he climbed the steps leading to a bright yellow caravan and knocked at the door.

The upper part of the door, being used as a window, was glass, behind which were two small muslin curtains tied back with pink ribbon. No one came to open the door when the old man knocked, and he was about to turn away when some boys called out to him, "Rap again, mister, rap again. There's a girl in there."

The old man thanked them, and rapped again at the caravan door.

A girl, about twelve years of age, appeared at the window. Her hair, which was of a rich auburn colour, was hanging down almost to her waist, and her eyes were the most beautiful the old man thought he had ever seen.

She was very poorly dressed, and she shivered as the damp, cold air rushed in through the open door.

"Good afternoon," said the old man.

The girl was just going to answer him when a loud fit of coughing caused her to look round. A voice said hurriedly, "Shut the door, Rosalie; it's so cold. Ask whoever it is to come in."

2

Rosalie

The old man did not wait for a second invitation. He stepped inside the caravan, and the girl called Rosalie closed the door.

At the end of the caravan was a narrow bed like a berth on board ship. On it a woman was lying who was evidently very ill. She was the girl's mother, the old man felt sure. She had the same beautiful eyes and sunny hair, though her face was thin.

There was not room for much furniture in the small caravan; a tiny stove (the chimney of which went through the wooden roof), a few pans, a shelf containing cups and saucers, and two boxes which served as seats. There was only just room for the old man to stand, and the fire was so near him that he was in danger of being scorched.

Rosalie seated herself on one of the boxes close to her mother's bed.

"You must excuse my intruding, ma'am," said the old man, with a polite bow; "but I've brought a picture, if your girl will accept it from me."

A flush of pleasure came into Rosalie's face as the man brought out of his pocket the promised gift. She seized it eagerly, and unrolled the paper with evident delight, whilst her mother raised herself on her elbow to look at it with her.

It was the picture of a shepherd, with a kind and loving face, who was sitting on a large rock, holding a lamb safely in his arms. Two other lambs were close to him, and to Rosalie they all appeared to be happy. Perhaps happiest of all was the shepherd, for he was looking down at the lamb in his arms. Underneath the picture were these words, printed in large letters: "Rejoice with me, for I have found my sheep which was lost. There is joy in the presence of the angels of God over one sinner that repenteth."

The Good Shepherd.

"Rejoice with Me, for I have found My sheep which was lost.
There is joy in the presence of the angels of God over one sinner that repenteth." St. Luke XV.

The girl read the words aloud in a very clear, distinct voice, as her mother gazed at the picture.

"Those are sweet words," said the old man.

"Yes," said the woman, with a sad smile; "I have heard them many times before."

"Has the Good Shepherd ever said them of *you*, ma'am? Has He ever called the bright angels together and said to them of *you*, 'Rejoice with me, for I have found my sheep which was lost'?"

The woman did not speak. A fit of coughing came on, and the old man stood looking at her thoughtfully.

"You are very ill, ma'am, I'm afraid," he said.

"Yes, very ill," replied the woman. "Everyone can see that but Augustus!" There was bitterness in her voice, the man thought.

"Augustus is my father," said the girl.

"No; *he* doesn't see it," continued the woman. "He thinks I ought to get up and act in the play, just as usual. I did try at the last place we went to; but I collapsed as soon as my part was over, and I've been in bed ever since."

"You must be tired of moving about, ma'am," said the old man, compassionately.

"Tired!" said she. "I should think I *am* tired! It isn't what I was brought up to do." She gave a very deep sigh. "It's a weary time I have of it—a weary time."

"Are you always on the move, ma'am?" asked the old man.

"All the summertime," said the woman. "We get into lodgings for a little time in the winter; and then we hire ourselves out to some of the small town theaters; but all the rest of the year we're going from fair to fair."

The girl climbed up on one of the boxes, and brought

down a square red pincushion from the shelf which ran round the top of the caravan. From this she took two pins, and fastened the picture on the wooden wall, so that her mother could see it as she was lying in bed.

"It looks good there," said the girl. "Mother, you can look at it easily now!"

"Yes, ma'am," said the old man, as he prepared to take his leave; "and as you look at it, think of that Good Shepherd who is seeking you. He wants to find you, and take you up in His arms, and carry you home. He won't mind what it has cost Him, if you'll only let Him do it."

The old man went carefully down the steps of the caravan. Rosalie stood at the window watching him pick his way to the other shows, to which he was carrying the same message. She looked out from between the muslin curtains until he disappeared to a distant part of the field. Then she turned to her mother and said eagerly, "It's a very interesting picture, isn't it, Mother?"

But no answer came from the bed. Rosalie thought her mother was asleep, and crept on tiptoe to her side, afraid of waking her. But she found her mother's face buried in the pillow, on which tears were falling. Rosalie sat beside her without moving, and kept gazing at her picture till she knew every line of it. And at last, her mother fell asleep with Rosalie's voice saying softly:

" 'Rejoice with me, for I have found my sheep which was lost. There is joy in the presence of the angels of God over one sinner that repenteth.' "

CHAPTER 2

The Traveling Theater

t was the next evening; the fair was once more in its glory, and crowded. The sideshows were again illuminated, and three rows of brilliant stars shone above the canvas theater which belonged to Rosalie's father, Augustus. He had been out all day, strolling about the town, and had only returned in time to make preparation for the evening's entertainment.

"Norah!" called Augustus to his wife, as he put his head in the door of the caravan, "surely you will come and take your part tonight?"

"I can't, Augustus, and you would know why, if you stayed with me long enough. I've been coughing nearly the whole day."

"Well, I wish you would get better soon. It's very awkward to have to fill your part every time."

"I'll come as soon as ever I can," said his wife.

"It's to be hoped you will!" replied her husband. "Women like you are always fancying they are ill. They lie thinking about it, and nursing themselves, long after a man would have been at his work again. It's half laziness, that's what it is!" said Augustus, fiercely.

"If you felt as ill as I do, Augustus," said his wife patiently, "I'm sure *you* wouldn't do *any* work."

"Hold your tongue!" said her husband. "I know better than that. Well, mind you have Rosalie ready in time; we shall begin early tonight."

Rosalie had crept to her mother's side, and was listening quietly to her father's rough words. There were tears in her eyes.

"Stop crying this minute, child!" said Augustus, harshly. "Wipe your eyes, you great baby! Do you think you'll be fit to come on the stage if your eyes are red and swollen from crying? Do you hear me? Stop at once!" he shouted, as he slammed the caravan door shut.

"Rosalie, darling," said her mother, "you mustn't cry. Your father will be angry, and it's time you got ready. What a noise there is in the fair already!" she added, holding her aching head.

Rosalie wiped her eyes and washed her face, and then brought out a dress from one of the boxes. It was the dress in which she was to act in the play—a white muslin dress, looped with pink roses, and there was a wreath of paper roses to wear in her hair. She dressed herself, and then went to her mother to have the wreath of roses fastened.

What a contrast Rosalie looked to the rest of the caravan!

8

The Traveling Theater

The shabby furniture and the dirty, torn dress she had just laid aside were quite out of keeping with the pretty white-robed figure now standing by the bed.

At length her father's voice called her, so after giving her mother a last kiss, and after placing some water on the box near her (in case a violent fit of coughing should come on), Rosalie ran quickly down the caravan steps and rushed to the brilliantly lighted tent which was the theater. A crowd of people stared at her as she flitted past and disappeared up the theater steps.

The audience had not yet been admitted, so Rosealie crept into the place behind the stage in which her father's company were assembled. They all looked tired and cross, for this was the last night of the fair, and they had received very little sleep whilst it lasted.

At length Augustus announced that it was time to begin, and they all went out upon a platform, just underneath the three rows of illuminated stars. Here they danced, and sang, and shook tambourines, in order to entice the people to enter. Then they disappeared within, and a crowd of eager spectators immediately rushed up the steps, paid their admission money, and took their seats.

As soon as the play was over the people rushed out into the fair to seek for fresh amusement. But the actors had no rest. Once more they appeared on the platform, to attract a fresh audience, and then the same play was repeated, the same songs were sung, the same words were said; fresh to the people who were listening, but stale and monotonous to the actors themselves!

And so it went on all night. As soon as one performance was over another began, and the theater was filled and refilled long after the clock of the neighbouring church had

9

struck the hour of twelve.

At last it was all over. The final audience had left, the brilliant stars disappeared, and Rosalie was able to creep back to her mother. So weary and exhausted was she, that she could hardly drag herself up the caravan steps. She opened the door very gently, that she might not disturb her mother, and then she tried to undress herself. But she was aching in every limb and, sitting down on the box beside her mother's bed, she fell asleep, her head resting on her mother's pillow.

In about an hour's time her mother woke, and she found Rosalie sleeping in her uncomfortable position, her white dress unfastened, and the pink roses from her hair fallen on the ground. Weak as she was, the girl's mother dragged herself out of bed to help her tired child to undress.

"Rosalie, dear," she said gently, "wake up."

But for some time Rosalie did not stir, and, when her mother touched her, she sat up, and said, as if in her sleep, " 'Rejoice with me, for I have found my sheep, which was lost.' "

"She is dreaming of her picture, poor child!" said her mother to herself.

Then Rosalie woke, and shivered as she felt the cold night air on her bare neck and arms. Very gently her mother helped her to take off her white dress and her small ragged petticoats; and then Rosalie crept into bed and into her mother's arms.

"Poor lamb!" said her mother as the girl lay against her.

"Am I the lamb?" asked Rosalie, in a sleepy voice. Her mother did not answer, but lay awake by her side, thinking, till the morning dawned.

CHAPTER 3

The Day After the Fair

THE next morning Rosalie was awakened by a rap at the caravan door. She crept out of bed and, putting her shawl over her shoulders, peeped out between the muslin curtains.

"It's Toby, Mother," she said. "I'll see what he wants."

She opened the door a crack, and Toby whispered, "Miss Rosie, we're going to start off in about half an hour. Master has just sent me for the horses. We've been up all night packing. Three of the wagons is loaded, and they've only some of the scenery to roll up, and then we shall start."

"Where are we going, Toby?" asked Rosalie.

11

"It's a long way off," said Toby. "We've never been there before, master says, and it will take us nearly a week. But I must be off, Miss Rosie, or master will be coming."

"Aren't you tired, Toby?" asked Rosalie.

Toby shrugged his shoulders, and said, with a broad grin, "I wonder if anyone in this concern is ever anything else *but* tired!"

Then he walked away into the town for the horses, which had been put up in the stables of an inn, and Rosalie returned to her mother. There were several things to be done before they could start. All the crockery had to be taken from the shelf and stowed away in a safe place, lest the jolting over the rough and uneven field should throw it down. Besides this, Rosalie had to get her mother's breakfast ready, that she might eat it in peace before the shaking of the caravan commenced.

When all was ready Rosalie stood at the window and looked out. The fair looked very different than it had done the night before. Most of the people had been up all night, taking their shows to pieces, and packing everything up. Though it was not yet nine o'clock, many of them had already left, and the field was half empty.

What little grass the field once possessed had entirely disappeared. The bare, uneven ground was thickly strewn with dirty pieces of paper, broken boxes, and old rags, which had been left behind by the show people. There was a quantity of orange peel and coconut and oyster shells, which had been thrown into the mud the night before. Very dirty and untidy and forlorn it looked, as Rosalie gazed from the door of the caravan.

A wagon jolted past, laden with the largest of the roundabouts; the wooden horses and painted elephants were peeping out from the waterproof covering which had been thrown over them. Then a large swing passed by, followed by the show of the giant and dwarf. These were followed by a pea-boiling stall, and the marionettes. A few minutes afterwards, the show of the horse and the performing seal set out on their way to the next fair.

All of these rattled past, and Rosalie watched them go out of sight. Then Toby returned with the horses. They were yoked to the wagons and to the caravans, and the little cavalcade set forth. The jolting over the rough ground was very great, and Rosalie felt sorry for her mother as she was shaken from side to side of her bed.

Outside the field, they had to wait a long time, for the road was completely filled by the numerous caravans of the wild-beast show, and no one could pass until they were gone.

The elephants were standing close to the pavement, now and again twisting their long trunks into the trees of the small gardens in front of the neighbouring houses. They would undoubtedly have broken the branches had not their keeper driven them off with his whip. A crowd of children was gathered round, feeding them with bread and biscuits and enjoying the delay of the show.

But Augustus became very impatient, for he had a long journey before him. So, after pacing up and down and complaining for some time, he went up to the manager of the wild-beast show. He used such unpleasant language that a policeman told him to keep the peace.

At length the huge circus caravans, each drawn by six strong horses, moved slowly on, led by a procession of elephants and camels, and followed by a large crowd of children, who accompanied them out to the edge of the town. Here, by turning down a side-street, the theater party was able to pass them, and thus get ahead of them on their journey.

Rosalie was glad to leave the town, and feel the fresh country air blowing upon her face. She opened the upper part of the door, and stood looking out, watching Toby, who was driving. She talked to him from time to time about the places which they passed. It was a new road to Rosalie and to her mother.

About twelve o'clock they came to a village, where they halted for a short time, that the horses might rest. The country children were just leaving the village school, and they gathered round the caravans with open eyes and mouths, staring curiously at the smoke coming from the small chimneys, and at Rosalie, who was looking out from between the muslin curtains. But, after satisfying their curiosity, they moved away in little groups to their various homes, that they might be in time to get their dinner before afternoon school.

When the village street was quiet, Rosalie stood at the door, watching the birds hop from tree to tree and the bees gathering honey from flowers in the gardens. Her mother was much better today, and was dressing herself slowly, for she thought that a breath of country air might revive and strengthen her.

Augustus, Toby, and the other men of the company had gone into the small inn for refreshment, and Toby was sent back to the caravan with large slices of bread and cheese for Rosalie and her mother. The girl ate it eagerly—the fresh air had given her an appetite—but her mother could not touch it. As soon as she was dressed she crept, with Rosalie's help, to the door of the caravan. There she sat on the top step, leaning against one of the boxes which her daughter had dragged from its place to make a support for her.

The caravan was drawn up by the side of a cottage. There was a small garden in front of it, filled with sweet flowers, large cabbage-roses, southernwood, rosemary, sweetbriar, and lavender. As the wind blew softly over them, it wafted their sweet fragrance to the sick woman sitting on the caravan steps. The quiet stillness of the country was very refreshing and soothing to her, after the turmoil and din of the fair. No sound was to be heard but the singing of the larks overhead, the humming of the bees, and the gentle rustling of the breeze amongst the branches.

Then the cottage door opened, and a little girl, about three years old, ran out with a ball in her hand. She rolled it down the path leading to the garden gate.

A minute afterwards a young woman brought her work outside, and, sitting on the seat near the cottage door, watched her child at play. She was knitting a little red sock for one of those tiny feet to wear. Click! click! click! went her knitting needles. But she kept her eyes on the child, ready to run to her at the first alarm, to pick her up if she should fall, or to soothe her if she should be in trouble.

Now and then she glanced at the caravan standing at her garden gate, and gave a look of pity at the poor, thin woman, whose cough from time to time was so distressing. Then, as was her custom, she began to sing as she worked. She had a clear voice, and Rosalie and her mother tried to listen. It seemed to be a hymn.

When the woman had finished singing, all was still again. There was hardly a sound except the pattering of the girl's feet on the garden path. But presently she began to cry, and her mother ran to her side to discover what had pained her.

It was only the loss of the ball, which she had thrown too high. It had gone over the hedge, and seemed to her lost forever.

The mother ran immediately to find it. But Rosalie had seen the ball come over the hedge, and heard the child's cry. When the mother appeared at the gate, she saw Rosalie returning from her chase after the ball, which had rolled some way down the hilly road. She brought it to the young mother, who thanked her for her kindness, and then gazed into Rosalie's face. She thought of the happy life her child led, compared with that of this poor wanderer. With this feeling in her heart, after restoring the ball to the once-more-contented child, she ran into the house, and returned with a mug of new milk, and a slice of bread spread with fresh country butter, which she handed to Rosalie and begged her to eat.

"Thank you," said Rosalie; "but please may my mother have it? I've had some bread and cheese, but she is too ill to eat that, and this would do her so much good."

"Yes, to be sure," said the kind-hearted countrywoman. "Give her that, and I'll fetch some more for you."

So Rosalie and her mother had quite a picnic on the steps of the caravan; with the young woman standing by, and talking to them as they ate, and now and then, looking over the hedge into the garden, to see if any trouble had come to her girl.

"I liked to hear you sing," said Rosalie's mother.

"Did you?" said the young woman. "I often sing when I'm knitting. My little one likes to hear me, and she almost knows that hymn now."

"I wish I knew it," said Rosalie.

"I'll tell you what," said the young woman, "I'll give you a card with it printed on. Our minister had it printed, and we've got two of them."

She ran again into the house, and returned with a card on which the hymn was printed in clear, distinct type. There were two holes pierced through the top of the card, and a piece of blue ribbon had been slipped through, and tied in a bow at the top. Rosalie seized it eagerly, and began reading it.

"We've got such a good minister here," said the young woman. "He has not been here more than a few months, and he has done so many things for us. His wife, Mrs. Leslie, reads aloud in one of the cottages once a week. We all take our work and go to listen to her, and she talks to us so beautiful out of the Bible. It always does me good to go."

She stopped suddenly, as she saw Rosalie's mother's face. She had turned deadly pale, and was leaning back against the box.

"What's the matter, ma'am?" said the kind-hearted woman. "I'm afraid you've turned faint; and how you tremble! Let me help you in. You'd better lie on your bed, hadn't you?"

She gave her her arm, and she and Rosalie took her inside the caravan, and laid her on her bed. But the lady was obliged to leave her in a minute or two, as her little girl was climbing on the gate, and she was afraid she would fall.

A few minutes afterwards a great noise was heard in the distance, and a number of the village children appeared, running in front of the wild-beast show, which was just passing through. The young woman took her little girl in her arms, and held her up, that she might see the elephants and camels, which were marching with stately dignity in front of the yellow caravans.

She watched them out of sight . . .

When they had gone, Toby appeared with the horse, and said his master had told him he was to start, and that he would follow presently with the rest of the wagons.

They were just leaving when the young woman gathered a bunch of flowers from her garden and handed them to Rosalie, saying, "Take them, and put them in water for your mother. Maybe the sight of them will do her good. You'll learn that hymn, won't you? Goodbye, and God bless you!"

She watched them out of sight, standing at her cottage gate with her child, whilst Rosalie leaned out of the window to wave to her and smile at her.

Then they turned a corner, and came into the main street of the village.

"Can you see the church, Rosalie?" asked her mother, hurriedly.

"Yes, Mother," said Rosalie; "it's just at the end of this street. It has trees all round it!"

"Are there any houses near?" asked her mother.

"Only one. A big house in a garden; but I can't see it very well, there are so many trees in front of it. It is the vicarage, I think."

"Ask Toby to put you down, Rosalie, and run and have a look at it as we pass."

So Rosalie was lifted down from the caravan, and ran up to the vicarage gate, whilst her mother raised herself on her elbow, to see as much as she could through the open window. But she could only see the spire of the church, and the chimneys of the house, and she was too exhausted to get up.

Presently Rosalie caught up with them, panting from running fast. Toby never dared to wait for her, lest his master should find fault with him for stopping. Rosalie often got down from the caravan to gather wild flowers, or to drink at a wayside spring and, as she was very fleet of foot, she was always able to catch up with them.

"What was it like, Rosalie?" asked her mother, when she was seated on the box beside her bed.

"Oh! ever so pretty. Such soft grass and such lovely roses, and a broad gravel walk right up to the door. And in the garden there was a lady; such a kind-looking lady. She was gathering some of the flowers with a girl about my age."

"Did they see you, Rosalie?"

"Yes; the girl saw me, peeping through the gate, and she said, 'Who is that girl, mama? I never saw her before.' And then her mother looked up and smiled at me; and she was just coming to speak to me when I turned frightened, because I saw our caravan had gone out of sight. So I ran away, and I've been running ever since to catch up with you."

The mother listened to Rosalie's account with a pale and restless face. Then she lay back on her pillow and sighed several times.

At last they heard a rumbling sound behind them, and Toby announced, "It's master; he's soon caught up with us!"

"Rosalie," said her mother, anxiously, "don't you ever tell your father about that house, or that I told you to go and look at it, or about what that young woman said. Mind you never say a word to him about it. Promise me, Rosalie."

"Why not, Mother?" asked Rosalie, with a very perplexed face.

"Never mind why, Rosalie," said her mother. "I don't wish it."

"Very well," said Rosalie.

"I'll tell you sometime, Rosalie," said her mother gently, a minute or two afterwards. "Not today, though. I can't tell it today."

Rosalie wondered very much what her mother meant. She sat watching the pale face as her mother lay on her bed with her eyes closed. What was she thinking about? What was it she would tell her? For some time Rosalie sat quite still, musing on what her mother had said, and then she pinned the card on the wall just over her new picture, and read the words of the hymn out loud.

After this she arranged the flowers in a small glass, and put them on the box near her mother's bed. The sweetbriar and cabbage roses and southernwood filled the caravan with their fragrance. Rosalie took up her usual position at the door, to watch Toby driving, and to see all that was to be seen by the way.

They passed through several other villages, and saw many lone farmhouses and solitary cottages. When night came, they drew up on the outskirts of a small market town. Toby took the horses to an inn, and they rested there for the night.

CHAPTER 4

Her Mother's Story

HE next morning, as soon as it was light, the horses were harnessed and the theater party proceeded on its way. Rosalie's mother seemed well. The country air had helped her recovery. She was able to dress herself and to sit on one of the boxes, gazing out at the green fields and clear blue sky. A fresh breeze came in at the open door and fanned her face and the face of the girl who sat beside her.

"Rosalie," said her mother, suddenly, "would you like to hear about the time when your mother was a girl?"

"Yes, please," said Rosalie, nestling up to her side. "I know nothing at all about it."

"No, Rosalie," said her mother; "it's the beginning of a

sad story, and I did not want you to know about it. But I sometimes think I shan't be long with you, and I had rather tell it to you myself than have anyone else tell it. And you're getting quite grown-up now, Rosalie. You will be able to understand many things you could not have understood before. Certain things the last few days have brought it all back to me and made me think of it by day, and dream of it by night."

"*Please* tell me, Mother," begged Rosalie.

"Then draw closer to me, child, for I don't want Toby to hear; and, mind, you must never speak of what I'm going to tell you before your father—*never!* Promise me, Rosalie," she said, earnestly.

"No, never, Mother," said Rosalie.

There was silence for a minute or two afterwards—no sound to be heard but the cracking of Toby's whip and the rumbling of the wagons.

"Aren't you going to begin?" asked Rosalie, at length.

"I almost wish I hadn't promised to tell you," said her mother, hurriedly. "It cuts me up so to think of it. But never mind; you ought to know, and you will know some day, so I'd better tell you myself. Rosalie, I was never born to this life of misery; I brought myself to it. I chose it," she said, bitterly; "and I'm only getting the harvest of what I sowed myself."

As she said this, she began to shiver from head to foot. Rosalie put her warm hand in her mother's cold one.

"So now, darling, I'll tell you all about it, just as if I was talking about someone else. I'll forget it is myself, or I shall never be able to tell it. I'll try and fancy I'm on the stage, and talking about the troubles of someone I never knew.

"I was born in a country village, in the south of England. We lived in a large house, which was built halfway up the

side of a wooded hill, and an avenue of beautiful, old trees
led up to the house. There was a large conservatory at one
side of it, filled with the rarest flowers. And in a shady
corner of the grounds my mother had a kind of grotto, with
lovely ferns, through which a clear stream of water was ever
flowing. This fernery was my mother's great delight, and
here she spent much of her time. She took very little notice
of her children; and when she was not in the garden, she was
generally lying on the sofa in the drawing room, reading.

"My father was a very different man. He was fond of his
children; but he was obliged to be away from home often, so
that we did not see as much of him as we should otherwise
have done.

"I had one brother and one sister. My brother was much
older than we were. My sister Lucy was a year younger than I
was. She was such a pretty child, and had a very sweet
disposition. When we were children we got on very well
together, and shared every pleasure and every grief. My
father bought us a little white pony; and on this we used to
ride in turns about the park when we were quite small
children, our old nurse following to see that no harm came
to us.

"Our old nurse was a very good woman. She taught us to
say our prayers night and morning, and on Sundays she used
to sit with us under a tree in the park, and show us Scripture
pictures, and tell us stories out of the Bible. There was one
picture of a shepherd, Rosalie. It came back to my mind the
other day when that old man gave it to you; only in mine the
shepherd was just drawing the lamb out of a deep, miry pit
into which it had fallen, and the text underneath it was this:
'The Son of man is come to seek and to save that which is
lost.' We used to learn these texts and repeat them to our

24

"We spent hours, dressing up, and pretending to be great ladies!"

nurse when we looked at the pictures.

"And after tea we used to sing one of our hymns and say our prayers, and then she took us in and put us to bed. I have often thought of those quiet, happy Sundays when I have been listening to the noise and racket of the fair.

"I had a very strong will, Rosalie, and even as a child I hated to be controlled. If I set my heart upon anything, I wanted to have it at once. I loved my dear, old nurse; but when we were about eight years old she had to leave us to live with her mother. My mother engaged a governess for us then, to teach us in the morning, and take us out in the afternoon. She was a lazy person, and she took very little trouble with us, and my mother did not see what we were doing. She was called Miss Manders. We learnt very little, and got into idle and careless ways. She used to sit down in the park with a book, and we were allowed to follow our own devices, and amuse ourselves as we pleased. When it rained, we spent hours, dressing up, and pretending to be grand ladies!

"When my brother Gerald came home, it was always a great cause of excitement to us. We used to meet him at the station, and drive him home in triumph. In these holidays Miss Manders went away, and Gerald used to amuse us with stories of his school friends, as we walked with him through the park. He was a very fine-looking lad, and my mother was very proud of him. She thought much more of him than of us, because he was a boy, and was to be the heir to the property. She like to drive out with her handsome son, who was admired by everyone who saw him, and sometimes we were allowed to go with them. We were generally left outside in the carriage, whilst Mama and Gerald called at the large houses of the neighbourhood. We used to jump out, as soon as they had disappeared inside the house, and explore the different gardens, and plan how we would lay out our grounds when we had houses of our own. But what's that, Rosalie? Has everyone stopped?"

Rosalie ran to the door and looked out.

"Yes, Mother," she said. "Father's coming!"

"Then mind, not a word," said her mother, in a hoarse whisper.

"Well!" said Augustus, entering the caravan in a theatrical manner, "I thought I might as well enjoy the happiness of the amiable society of my lady and her daughter!"

This was said with a profound bow towards his wife and Rosalie. He called to Toby to start off again.

"Glad to see you so much better, madam," he continued. "Rather strange, isn't it, that your health and spirits have revived immediately we have left the scene of public action, or—to speak in plain terms—when there's no *work* to do?"

"I think it's the fresh air, Augustus, that has done me good. There was such a close, stifling smell from the fair, I felt worse directly we got there."

"It's to be hoped," he said, with a forced smile on his face, "that this resuscitation of the vital powers may be continued until we arrive at Lesborough. But the probability is that the moment we arrive on the scene of action you will be seized with that most unpleasant of all maladies, distaste to your work, and will be compelled once more to resume that most interesting and pathetic occupation of playing the invalid!"

"Oh! Augustus, don't speak to me like that!" said his wife.

Augustus made no answer, but taking a piece of paper from his pocket, twisted it up, and, putting it into the fire, lighted a long pipe and began to smoke. The smoke of the tobacco brought on his wife's cough, but he took very little notice of her, except to ask her occasionally, between the whiffs of his pipe, how long that melodious sound was to last. Then his eyes fell upon Rosalie's picture, which was pinned to the side of the caravan.

"Where did you get *that* from?" he inquired, turning to his wife.

"It's mine, Father," said Rosalie. "An old gentleman in the fair gave it to me."

"It will do for a *child!*" he said, scornfully. "Toby, what are you doing? You're creeping along; we shall never get there at *this* pace!"

"The horse is tired, master," said Toby. "He's had a long stretch these two days."

"Beat him then. Flog him well! Do you think I can afford to waste time upon the road? The wild beasts are a mile ahead, at the very least, and the marionettes will be there by this time. We shall arrive when all the people have spent their money!"

There was one subject of standing dispute between Toby and his master. Toby hated to see the horses overworked, ill-fed and badly used. He was always remonstrating about it, and thereby bringing down upon himself his master's wrath and abuse. Augustus cared nothing for the comfort or welfare of those under him. To get as much work as possible out of them, and to make as much money by them as he could, was all he thought of. They might be tired, or hungry, or overburdened; what did it matter to him?

Toby refused to beat the poor, tired horse, which was already straining itself. The additional weight of Augustus had been very trying to it the last few miles.

When Augustus saw that Toby did not mean to obey him,

he sprang to the door of the caravan in a rage, seized the whip from Toby's hand, and then beat the poor horse unmercifully, causing it to start from side to side, till nearly everything in the caravan was thrown to the ground. Rosalie and her mother trembled with indignation and horror.

Then, with one last tremendous blow, aimed at Toby's head, Augustus threw down the whip, and returned to his pipe.

CHAPTER 5

Rosalie's First Sermon

THE next morning, as soon as they had started on their journey, Rosalie begged her mother to continue her story. So, after satisfying herself that her husband was not close by, Rosalie's mother took up the thread of the story from where she had left it when they were interrupted the day before.

"I was telling you, dear, about my life in that quiet country manor house. I think I can remember nothing further worth mentioning, until an event happened which altered the whole course of our lives.

"Lucy and I had been out riding in the park on the beautiful new horses which our father had given us a few months before, and we had had a very pleasant afternoon.

I can see Lucy now in her riding-habit—her fair hair hanging down her back, and her cheeks glowing with the air and exercise. She was very pretty, was my sister Lucy. People said I was handsomer than she was, and had a better figure and brighter eyes; but Lucy was a sweet-looking little thing, and no one could look at her without loving her.

"We got down from our horses, leaving them with the groom who had been riding out with us, and ran into the house. But we were met by one of the maids. Her face was white with alarm and she begged us to go quietly upstairs, as our father was very ill and the doctor said he was to be perfectly quiet. We asked her what was the matter with him. She told us he had been riding home from the railway station, and his horse had thrown him, and that he had been brought home unconscious. More than this she could not tell us, but our mother came into our bedroom, and told us, with more feeling than I had ever seen in her face before, that our father could not live much longer.

"I shall never forget that night. I lay awake, listening to the hall clock as it struck one hour after another. Then I crept out of bed, and put my head out of the window. It was a close night—not a breath seemed to be stirring. I wondered what was going on in the next room, and whether I should ever see my father again. Then I thought I heard a sound, but it was only Lucy sobbing beneath the bedclothes.

" 'Lucy,' I said, glad to find she was awake, 'isn't it a long night?'

" 'Yes, Norah,' she answered. 'I'm so frightened. Do you have a light?'

"I found the matches and lighted a candle; but three or four large moths darted into the room, so I had to close the window.

31

"We lay awake in our beds watching the moths darting in and out of the candle flame, and straining our ears for any sound from our father's room. Each time a door shut we jumped and sat up in bed, listening.

" 'Norah, do you think you would go to Heaven if you were to die?' asked Lucy suddenly.

" 'Yes, of course,' I said, quickly. 'Why do you ask me?'

" 'I don't think I should,' said Lucy. 'I'm almost sure I shouldn't.'

"We lay still for another hour, and then the door opened and our mother came in. She was crying, and had a handkerchief to her eyes.

" 'Your father wants to see you,' she said. 'Come at once.'

"We crept very quietly into our father's room, and stood beside his bed. His face was so changed that it frightened us. But he held out his hand to us, Rosalie, and we drew closer to him. Then he whispered:

" 'Goodbye! don't forget your father; and don't wait till you come to die to get ready for another world.'

"Then we kissed him, and our mother told us to go back to bed. I never forgot my father's last words to us; and I often wondered what made him say them.

"The next morning we heard that our father was dead. My brother Gerald arrived too late to see him. He was at college then, and was just preparing for his last examinations.

"My mother seemed at first very distressed by my father's death. She shut herself up in her room, and would see no one. The funeral was a very grand one. All the people of the neighborhood came to it, and Lucy and I peeped out of one of the top windows to see it start.

"After it was over, Gerald went back to college, and my

mother returned to her books. I think she thought, Rosalie, that she would be able to return to her old life much as before. But no sooner had Gerald passed his last examinations than she received a letter from him stating he intended to be married in a few months, and would bring his bride to the Hall. Then for the first time the truth flashed upon my mother's mind, that she would soon be no longer the mistress of the manor house, but would have to seek a home elsewhere.

"She seemed at first very angry with Gerald for marrying so early; but she could say nothing against his choice, for she was a young lady of title, and one in every way suited to the position she was to occupy.

"My mother at length decided to move to a town in the midland counties, where she would have some good society and plenty of excitement, as soon as her mourning for my father was ended.

"It was very sad for us, leaving the old home. Lucy and I went round the park the day before we left, gathering leaves from our favorite trees, and taking a last look at the home of our childhood. Then we walked through the house, and looked out of the windows on the lovely wooded hills with eyes which were full of tears. I have never seen it since, and I'm sure I shall never see it again. Sometimes, when we are coming through the country, it brings it back to my mind, and I could almost fancy I was walking down one of the long grassy terraces, or wandering in the quiet shade of the trees in the park. Hush! what was that, Rosalie?" said her mother, leaning forward to listen. "Was it music?"

At first Rosalie could hear nothing, except Toby whistling to his horse, and the rumbling of the wheels of the bright, yellow caravan. She went to the door and leaned out, and listened once more. The sun was beginning to set, for Rosalie's mother had only been able to talk at intervals during the day, from her frequent fits of coughing, and from numerous other interruptions, such as the preparations for dinner, the halting to give the horses rest, and the occasional visits of Augustus.

Clouds were gathering in the west, as the evening breeze wafted to the girl's ears the distant sound of bells.

"It's bells, Mother," she said, turning round. "Church bells; can't you hear them? Ding-dong bell, ding-dong bell."

"Yes," said her mother. "I can hear them clearly now. Our old nurse used to tell us they were saying, 'Come and pray, come and pray.' Oh! Rosalie, it is such a comfort to be able to speak of those days to someone! I've kept it all hidden up in my heart till sometimes I have felt as if it would burst."

"I can see the church now," said Rosalie. "We're going through the village, aren't we, Toby?"

"Yes, Miss Rosie," said Toby. "We're going to stop there tonight. The horses are tired out, and it's so plain to see, that even the master can see it now. We shall get on all the quicker for giving them a bit of rest."

By the time they reached the village, it was growing dark, and the country people were lighting their candles, and gathering round their small fires. Rosalie could see inside many a cheerful home, where the firelight was shining on the faces of the father, the mother, and the children.

Ding-dong bell, ding-dong bell; still the chimes went on, and one and another came out of the small cottages, and took the road leading to the church, with books under their arms.

Toby drove on. Nearer and nearer the chines sounded until, at last, just as the caravan reached a wide open green in front of the church, they ceased, and Rosalie saw the last person entering the church door before the service began.

The wagons and caravans were drawn up on this open space for the night. Toby and the other men led the horses away to the stables of the inn. Augustus followed them, to enjoy himself amongst the lively company. Rosalie and her mother were left alone.

"Mother," said Rosalie, as soon as the men had turned the corner, "may I go and peep at the church?"

"Yes, child," said her mother; "only don't make a noise if people are inside."

Rosalie darted across the common, and opened the church gate. The gravestones looked very solemn in the twilight. She went quickly past them and crept along the side of the church to one of the windows. Rosalie could see the inside of the church quite well, because it was lighted up; but no one could see her as she was standing in the dark churchyard. Her bright, quick eyes soon took in all that was to be seen. The minister was kneeling down, and so were all the people. There were a good many there, though the church was not full, as it was the mid-week service.

Rosalie watched at the window until all the people got up from their knees, when the minister announced a hymn, and they began to sing. Rosalie looked for the door, that she might hear the music better. It was a warm evening, and the door was open. Before she knew what she was about she had crept inside, and was sitting on a seat just within. Rosalie enjoyed the singing, and when it was over the minister began to speak. He had a clear, distinct voice, and he spoke in simple language which everyone could understand.

Rosalie listened with all her might. It was the first church sermon she had ever heard. "The Son of man is come to seek and to save that which is lost." That was the text of Rosalie's first sermon.

As soon as the service was over she stole out of the church, and crept down the dark churchyard. She had passed through the gate and was crossing the village green to the caravan before the first person had left the church. To Rosalie's joy, her father had not returned; for he had found the company in the village inn extremely attractive. Rosalie's mother looked up.

"Where have you been all this time, Rosalie?"

Rosalie gave an account of all she had seen, and told her how she had crept in at the open door of the church.

"And what did the minister say?" asked her mother.

"He said those words on your picture: 'The Son of man is come to seek and to save that which is lost.' "

"And what did he tell you about it?"

"He said Jesus went up and down all over to look for lost sheep. And he said that we were the sheep, and Jesus was looking for *us*. Do you think He is looking for you and me?"

"I don't know. I suppose so," said her mother; *"I* shall take a great deal of looking for, I'm afraid."

"But he said, Mother, that if only we would *let* Him find us, He would be sure to do it. He doesn't mind *how* much trouble He takes about it!"

Rosalie's mother was quite still for some time after this. Rosalie stood at the caravan door, watching the bright stars coming out one by one in the still sky.

"Mother dear," she said. "is *He* up there?"

"Who, Rosalie, child?" asked her mother.

"The Savior. Is He up in one of the stars?"

"Well, Heaven's somewhere, Rosalie. Perhaps it *is* beyond the sky."

"Would it be any good telling Him?"

"Telling Him what, dear?"

"Just telling Him that you and me want seeking and finding."

"I don't know, Rosalie; you can try," said her mother sadly.

"Please, Good Shepherd," said Rosalie, looking up at the stars, "come and seek me and Mother, and find us very quick, and keep us very safe, like the lamb in the picture."

"Will that do?" asked Rosalie, after a pause.

"Yes," said her mother. "I think it will." And she sounded almost relieved that the prayer had been said.

CHAPTER 6

A Family Secret

ow pleasant the village looked the next morning, when Rosalie woke and looked out of the caravan. She was quite sorry to leave, but there was no rest for the wanderers. They must move on towards the town where they were to perform next. As they traveled, Rosalie's mother went on with her story.

"I told you, darling, that my mother took a house in town, that we all moved there, and that my brother Gerald might take possession of our old home. We were getting older now, and my mother finally sent Miss Manders away, and left us to our own devices.

"My sister Lucy had been very different since our father died. She was so quiet. I often wondered what was the matter with her. She spent nearly all her time in a little attic

38

room which she called her secret place. I did not know why she went there, till one day I went upstairs to get something out of a box, and found Lucy sitting in the window seat reading her Bible. I asked her what she read it for, and she said, " 'Oh! Norah, it makes me so happy. Won't you come and read it with me?' But I tossed my head, and said I had too much to do to waste my time like that; and I ran downstairs, and tried to forget what I had seen, for I knew that my sister was right and I was wrong. Oh, Rosalie, I've often thought that, if I had listened to my sister that day, what a different life I might have led!

"Well, I must go on; I'm coming to the saddest part of my story, and I want to get over it as quickly as I can.

"It has to do with a family of the name of Roehunter. They were rich people, friends of my mother. Miss Georgina and Miss Laura Roehunter were very dashing girls. They took a great fancy to me, and we were always together. They were passionately fond of the theater, and they took me to it night after night.

"I could think of nothing else, Rosalie. I dreamt of it every night. It took hold of me. I admired the scenery; I admired the actors; I admired everything that I saw. I thought if I was only on the stage I should be perfectly happy. There was nothing in the world I wanted so much. It seemed to me such a free, happy, romantic life. When an actress was greeted with bursts of applause I envied her. How wearisome my life seemed when compared with hers!

"I determined that, as soon as possible, I would have a change, cost what it might. Soon after this the Roehunters told me that they were going to put on their own play at home, and that I must come and help them. It was just what I wanted. Now, I thought, I could fancy myself as a *real* actress!

"They engaged some professional actors from the theater to teach us our parts, to arrange the scenery, and to help us to do everything in the best possible manner. I had to go up to the Roehunters' house again and again to learn my part for the performance. And there it was, Rosalie, that I met your father. You see, he was one of the actors they employed.

"You can guess what came next, darling. Your father saw how well I could act. By degrees he found out I should like to do it always, instead of leading my humdrum life at home. So he used to meet me in the street and talk to me about it, and he told me that, if I would only come with him, I should have a life of pleasure and excitement, and never know what care was. Then he arranged that we should run away and be married.

"Oh! darling, I shall never forget that day. I arrived home late at night, or rather early in the morning, worn out with the evening's entertainment. I had been much praised for the way I had performed my part, and some of the company had declared I should make a first-rate actress, and I thought to myself they little knew how soon I was to become one! As I drove home, I felt in a perfect whirl of excitement. The day had come at last. Was I glad? I hardly knew; I tried to think I was; but somehow I felt sick at heart. I could not shake that feeling off, and as I walked upstairs I felt miserable.

"My mother had gone to bed. I never saw her again. Lucy was fast asleep, lying with her hand under her cheek. I stood a minute or two looking at her. Her Bible was lying beside her, for she had been reading it the last thing before she went to sleep. Oh! Rosalie, I would have given anything to change places with Lucy then. But it was too late. Augustus was to meet me outside the house, and we were to be married at a church in the town that very morning.

"I turned away from Lucy, and began putting some things together to take with me, and I hid them under the bed lest Lucy should wake and see them. It was no use going to bed, for I had not got home from the theatricals till three o'clock, and in two hours Augustus would come. So I scribbled a note to my mother, telling her that when she received it I would be married, and that I would call and see her in a few days. Then I put out the light, lest it should wake my sister, and sat waiting in the dark.

"Before long I felt frightened. I almost determined to write Augustus a note saying I could not go through with it, but I thought he would laugh at me for being such a coward. So, I tried to picture to myself once more how fine it would be to be a real actress, and be always praised as I had been last night.

"At last the church clock struck five, so I took my bag from under the bed, wrapped myself up in a warm shawl, and leaving my note on the dressing table, prepared to go downstairs. But I turned back when I got to the door, to look once more at my sister Lucy. And, Rosalie, as I looked I felt as if my tears would choke me. I wiped them hastily away, however, and crept downstairs. Every creaking board made me jump and tremble lest I should be discovered. At every turning I expected to see someone watching me. But no one appeared. I got down safely. Cautiously unbolting the hall door, I stole quietly out into the street, and soon found Augustus, who carried my bag under his arm, and that morning we were married.

"And then my troubles began. It was not half as pleasant being an actress as I had thought it would be. I did not know how tired I should be, nor what a comfortless life I should lead.

41

"Oh! Rosalie, I was soon sick of it. I would have given worlds to be back in my old home. I would have given worlds to lead that quiet, peaceful life again. I was praised and applauded in the theater, but after a time I cared very little for it. As for the acting itself, I became thoroughly sick of it. Rosalie dear, I have often fallen asleep, unable to undress myself from weariness after acting in the plays. Again and again I have wished that I had never seen the inside of a theater!"

"We stayed for some time in the town where my mother lived, for Augustus and I found work in a theater there. We had miserable lodgings, and often were very badly off. I called at home a few days after I was married. The servant shut the door in my face, saying that my mother never wished to see me again, or to hear my name mentioned. I used to walk up and down outside, trying to catch a glimpse of my sister Lucy; but she was never allowed to go out alone, and I could not get an opportunity of speaking to her. All my old friends passed me in the street—even the Roehunters would take no notice of me whatever.

"And then your father lost his work at the theater, and we left the town. Then I began to know what poverty meant. We traveled from place to place, sometimes getting occasional jobs at small town theaters, sometimes stopping at a town for a few months, and then being dismissed, and traveling on for weeks without hearing of any employment.

"It was then your little brother was born. Such a fine baby he was, and I named him Arthur after my father. I was very, very poor when he was born, and I could hardly get clothes for him to wear, but oh, Rosalie, I loved him very much. I wrote to my mother to tell her about it, and that the baby was named after my father. But she sent back my letter unread, and I never wrote to her again. Then one day, when I took up a newspaper, I saw my mother's death in it. I heard afterwards that she said I was not to be told of her death till after the funeral, for I had been a disgrace and a shame to the family. And that, they said, was the only time that she mentioned me after I ran away.

"My sister Lucy wrote me a very kind letter, and sent me some presents. But I was sorry afterwards, for your father kept writing to her for money, and telling her long tales about the distress I was in, to make her send us more.

"She often sent us money; but I felt as if I could not bear to take it. And she used to write me such beautiful letters—to beg me to find Jesus, and to remember what my father had said to us when he died. She said Jesus had made *her* happy, and would make *me* happy too. I often think now of what she said, Rosalie.

"Well, after a time I heard that Lucy had married a clergyman, and your father heard it too, and he kept writing to her and asking her for money again and again. At last came a letter from her husband, in which he said that he was very sorry to have to tell us that his wife could do no more for us. He requested that no more letters on the subject of money be sent, as they would receive no reply.

"Your father wrote again; but they did not answer it, and since then they have left the town where they were living, and he lost all clue to them. Rosalie, I hope he will never find them. I cannot bear to be a nuisance to my sister Lucy—my dear sister Lucy.

"As for Gerald, he has taken no notice of us at all. Your father has written to him from time to time, but his letters have always been returned to him.

"Well, so we went on, getting poorer and poorer. Once

your father took a job as postmaster in a small country village, and a lady there was very kind to me. She used to come and see my Arthur. He was very delicate, and at last he took a dreadful cold, and it settled on his chest, and my poor little lamb died. And, Rosalie darling, when I buried him under a little willow tree in that country churchyard, I felt as if I had nothing left to live for.

"We did not stay in that village long. We were neither of us used to keeping accounts, and we got the work at the post office in a complete muddle. So I had to leave the only home we ever had.

"Then your father fell in with a strolling actor, who was in the habit of frequenting fairs. And between them, by selling our furniture and almost everything we possessed, they bought some scenery and a caravan, and started a traveling theater. And when the man died, Rosalie, he left his share of it to your father.

"So for the last twelve years I've been moving about from place to place, just as we are doing now. And in this caravan, my girl, you were born.

"So now I've told you all I need tell you at present. Perhaps some day I shall talk about this again, but you will have some idea now why I am sometimes so very, very sad."

"Oh Mother!" said Rosalie. "I never knew!"

"It's all my own fault, child," said her mother. "I've brought it all upon myself, and I've no one but myself to blame."

"Poor, poor Mother," said Rosalie gently.

Then the sick woman seemed quite exhausted, and lay upon her bed for some time without speaking or moving. Rosalie sat by the door of the caravan, and sang softly to herself from the words on the card.

A Family Secret

Jesus, I Thy face am seeking,
Early will I come to Thee.
Words of love Thy voice is speaking:
"Come, come to me."

"Oh! Rosalie," said her mother, looking round. "*I* didn't come to Him early. Oh, if I only had! Mind *you* do, Rosie! It's so much easier for you now than when you get to be older like me."

"Why don't *you* come *now*, Mother?"

"I don't know. I don't expect He would take me; I have been such a sinner! There are other things, child, I have not told you about; and they are all coming back to my mind now. I don't know how it is, Rosalie, I never thought so much of them before."

"Perhaps the Good Shepherd is beginning to find you."

"Rosalie," said her father's voice, at the door of the caravan, "come into the next wagon. We've a new play, and you have your part to learn. Come away!"

So Rosalie had to leave her mother. And instead of singing the remainder of the hymn, she had to repeat again and again the words which she would say in the new play. Over and over again she repeated them, till she was weary of their very sound, her father scolding her if she made a mistake, or failed to give each word its proper emphasis.

When Rosalie was free it was time to get tea ready. They halted for the night at a small market town, just eight miles from Lesborough. It was in Lesborough that they were to perform next. They would enter it the next morning.

That night Rosalie lay awake and thought about the Good Shepherd. The moon was bright, and shone on her picture pinned to the wall.

CHAPTER 7

The Circus Procession

T was a fresh, sunshiny morning when the theater party reached Lesborough. Not a cloud was in the sky. Augustus was in fine spirits, for he thought that if the good weather lasted, his profits would be larger than usual.

On the road leading to the town they saw several small shows bound for the same destination. There was a show each of "The Lancashire Lass," "The Exhibition of the Performing Little Pigs," "Roderick Polglaze's Living Curiosities," and "The Show of the Giant Horse." Augustus knew the proprietor of nearly every caravan, and they exchanged greetings by the way, and congratulated each other on the fine weather which seemed to be before them.

As they drew near the town, they heard a tremendous

noise in the distance. In the main street a cloud of dust was in front of them, and an immense crowd of people. Rosalie and her mother came to the door of the caravan and looked out.

Presently the dust cleared away, and showed them a procession of glittering, gilded carriages coming towards them. It was surrounded by throngs of boys and girls, and men and women.

"What is it, Toby?" asked Rosalie.

"It's a large circus, Miss Rosie. Master said they were going to be here, and he was afraid they would draw a good many people off from us."

The theater party had to draw up on one side of the street to let the long procession pass.

First came a gilded carriage filled with musicians. They were playing a noisy tune. This was followed by about a dozen men on horseback, some dressed in shining armor, as knights of the olden time, and others as cavaliers of the time of the Stuarts.

Then came another large, gilded carriage on the top of which was a golden dragon, with colored reins round its neck. These were held by an old man, dressed as an ancient Briton, and supposed to represent St. George. Then came four horses ridden by ladies, dressed in brilliant velvet costumes. One was green, one red, one yellow, one violet. Each of them held long reins, which were fastened to the spirited piebald horses on which they rode.

Behind them came a man riding on two ponies, standing with one leg on each, and going at a great pace. Two girls and a young boy passed on three ponies, and next a tiny carriage, drawn by four little cream-colored horses, and driven by a boy dressed as the Lord Mayor's coachman.

Then came an exciting succession of clowns, riding, or standing on donkeys, and dressed in bright costumes. Then four very tall and fine horses, led by grooms in scarlet.

And lastly, an enormous gilded carriage drawn by six piebald horses, with colored flags on their heads. High on the top of this carriage sat a girl, dressed as Britannia. She was in white, with a scarlet scarf across her shoulders, a helmet on her head, and a trident in her hand. She was leaning against two large shields, which alone prevented her from falling from the great height.

Some way below, in front of the carriage, sat her two maidens, dressed in glittering silver tinsel (upon which the rays of the sun were dazzling). Behind her, clinging on to the back of the carriage, were two iron-clad men, whose armor was also shining brightly.

Then the procession was past, and there was nothing to be heard or seen but a noisy rabble, who were hurrying on to get another glimpse of the wonderful sight.

There were some girls standing near the caravan, close to Rosalie and her mother, as the circus procession passed. They were perfectly enraptured with all they saw. When Britannia came in sight they could hardly contain themselves, so envious were they of her. One of them told the other she would give *anything* to be sitting up there, dressed in gold and silver, and she thought Britannia must be as happy as Queen Victoria!

"Oh!" said Rosalie's mother, leaning out and speaking in a low voice. "Did you not think the girl looked unhappy? *You* would *soon* get tired of it!"

"Not I," said the girl. "I only wish I had the chance!"

Rosalie's mother smiled, and said to Rosalie, "This life is not always as exciting as it seems."

Nothing further happened until the theater party reached the place where the fair was to be held. It was to be in a large open square in the middle of the town, which was generally used as a marketplace.

Although it was only Saturday morning, and the fair was not to begin until Monday, many of the shows had already arrived. The marionettes and the wild beast show had completed their arrangements, and one of the roundabouts was already in action. From time to time its proprietor rang a large bell, to call together a fresh company of riders.

The children had no school, as it was Saturday, and they rushed home and clamored for pennies, to spend in sitting on a wooden horse, or elephant, or camel, or in one of the small omnibuses or open carriages, and then being taken round by means of steam at a tremendous pace, till their breath was nearly gone; and when they alighted once more on the ground, they hardly knew where they were, or whether they were standing on their heads or on their feet! Many of these children would then be dizzy and sick, and feel as if they were walking on ground which gave way beneath them as they trod on it!

As soon as Augustus arrived at the place where the theater was to be erected, he and his men began their work. For the next few hours there was nothing to be heard on all sides but rapping and hammering. Everyone worked with all his might to get everything finished before sunset. Each half hour fresh shows arrived, had their ground measured out for them by the marketkeeper, and then began to unload and fasten up immediately.

Rosalie stood at the door and looked out. She had seen it all so often before that it was no pleasure to her, and she felt very relieved as, one by one, the shows were finished and the hammering ceased. She was worried for her mother.

That night Augustus came into the caravan to smoke his pipe. He informed his wife it was very well she was so much better, for he and one of the actresses had had a disagreement, and she had taken her things and gone off, so of course Rosalie's mother would *have* to take her part on Monday night.

Rosalie looked at her mother, and Rosalie's mother looked at her, but neither of them spoke. But as soon as her father had left them for the night Rosalie said, "Mother, you'll *never* be able to stand on the stage all that long, long time. I'm sure it will make you worse."

"Never mind, Rosalie; it's no use telling your father. He thinks I am only complaining if I do."

"But, Mother, what if if makes you bad again, as it did before?"

"It can't be helped, child. I shall have to do it, so it's no use talking about it. I may as well do it without making a fuss. Your father is put out tonight, darling, and it would never do to annoy him more."

But Rosalie was not satisfied. She looked tearfully at her mother; and the next morning she went to tell her father that she did not think her mother would ever get through her part, she was too weak for it. But he told her shortly to mind her own business. So Rosalie could do nothing more, except watch her mother very carefully and gently all that long Sunday.

The church bells chimed in all directions. Crowds of people in their Sunday clothes passed along the marketplace to church or chapel.

It was a fine, bright day, so most of the showpeople were roaming about the town. Rosalie's mother was too weak to go out, and her daughter did not like to leave her.

"Rosalie," said her mother, that Sunday afternoon, "I'm going to give you a present."

"A present?" asked Rosalie in surprise.

"Yes, my girl. Pull that large box from under the bed. It's rather heavy. Can you manage it?"

"Oh yes, Mother, quite well."

Rosalie's mother sat down by the box, and began to unpack it. At the top of the box were some of her clothes and Rosalie's; but it was a long time since she had turned out the things at the bottom of the box. She took out from it a small bundle pinned up in a towel. Then, calling Rosalie to her side, she drew out the pins one by one, and opened it. Inside were several packages carefully tied up in paper.

In the first was a little pair of blue shoes, with two tiny, red socks.

"Those were my little Arthur's, Rosalie," said her mother. "I put them away the day he died, and I've never liked to part with them. No one will care for them when I'm gone, though," she said, with a sigh.

"Oh, Mother," said Rosalie, "don't talk so!"

The next packet contained a small, square box; but before Rosalie opened it her mother went to the door and looked cautiously out. Then, after seeing that no one was near, she took out of the velvet-lined case a beautiful little locket. There was a circle of pearls all round it, and the letters N.E.H. were engraved in a monogram on the outside.

Then she opened the locket, and showed Rosalie the colored miniature portrait of a girl with a sweet and gentle face, and large, soft brown eyes.

"Rosalie, darling," said her mother, "that is my sister Lucy."

Rosalie took the locket in her hand, and looked at it without saying a word.

"Yes," said the sick woman, "that is my sister Lucy—my own sister Lucy. I haven't looked at it for many a day. I can hardly bear to look at it now, for I am sure I shall never see her again. Who's that, Rosalie?" she said, covering the locket with her apron, as someone passed the caravan.

"It's only some men strolling through the fair," said Rosalie.

"I wouldn't have your father see this for the world. He would soon sell it if he did. I've hidden it all these years, and never let him find it. I could not bear to part with it. My sister Lucy gave it to me on the last birthday that I had at home. I remember it so well, Rosalie dear. I had been very unpleasant to Lucy for a long time before that. I knew I was doing wrong and I had such a weight on my mind that I could not shake it off, and it made me cross and irritable.

"Lucy was never cross with me. She always spoke gently and kindly to me; and I sometimes even wished she would be angry so that I might have some excuse for my bad behavior!

"Well, dear, when I woke that morning I found this little box laid on my pillow, and a note with it from Lucy. She asked me to always keep it for her sake. Rosalie darling, wasn't it good of her when I had been so bad to her?

"Well, I kissed her, and thanked her for it, and I wore it round my neck. When I ran away, I put it safely in my bag, and I've kept it ever since. Your father has not seen it for many years, and he has forgotten all about it. When we were so poor, I used to be afraid he would remember this locket and sell it, as he did all my other jewels. It was hard enough parting with some of them; but I did not care so much so long as I kept this one, for I promised Lucy that morning that I would *never, never* part with it."

"It is very pretty," said Rosalie.

"Yes, child; it will be yours some day—when I die. Remember, it is for you. But you must never let it be sold or pawned, Rosalie. I couldn't bear to think it ever would be. And now we'll put it back again. It won't be safe here; your father might come in any minute."

"Here's one more parcel, Mother."

"Yes, keep that out, dear; that's your present," said her mother. "I can't give you the locket yet, but you shall have the other today."

She took off the paper, and put into Rosalie's hands a small, black Bible. The girl opened the book, and read on the flyleaf, "Mrs. Augustus Joyce. From her friend Mrs. Bernard, in remembrance of Arthur, and with the prayer that she may meet her child in Heaven."

"I promised her I would read it, Rosalie; but I haven't. I read a few verses the first week she gave it to me, but I've never read it since. But now, I wish I had—oh, I wish I had!"

"Let *me* read it to you," suggested Rosalie.

"That's what I got it out for, darling. You must read a bit of it to me every day."

"Shall I begin at once, Mother?"

"Yes, Rosalie. I'll just write your name in it, that you may always remember your mother when you see it."

So Rosalie brought her a pen and ink, and she wrote at the bottom of the page, "My Rosalie, with her mother's love."

"And now, child, you may begin to read."

"What shall I read?"

"Find the part about your picture, dear. I should think it will say under the text where it is."

With some trouble Rosalie found Luke, chapter 15, and began to read verses three to seven: "And He spake this parable unto them, saying, What man of you, having an hundred sheep, if he lose one of them, doth not leave the ninety and nine in the wilderness, and go after that which is lost, until he find it? And when he hath found it, he layeth it on his shoulders, rejoicing. And when he cometh home, he calleth together his friends and neighbours, saying unto them, Rejoice with me; for I have found my sheep which was lost. I say unto you, that likewise joy shall be in heaven over one sinner that repenteth, more than over ninety and nine just persons, which need no repentance."

"*I* need repentance, Rosalie," said her mother.

"What is repentance?" asked Rosalie.

"It means being sorry for what you've done, darling, and hating yourself for it, and wishing never to do wrong again."

"Then, Mother, if you need repentance, you must be like the *one* sheep, *not* like the ninety-nine."

"Yes, child. I'm a lost sheep; there's no doubt about that. I've gone very far astray—so far that I don't suppose I shall ever get back again. It's much easier to get wrong than to get right. It's a *very, very* hard thing to find the right road when you've once missed it. It doesn't seem much use in my trying to get back; I have such a long way to go."

"But, Mother, isn't it just like the sheep?" Rosalie sounded excited.

"What do you mean, Rosalie darling?"

"Why, the sheep couldn't find its way back, could it? Sheep never can find their way. And this sheep didn't walk back, did it? He carried it on His shoulder. I don't suppose it would seem so very far when He carried it."

Rosalie's mother made no answer when her daughter

said this; but she seemed to be thinking about it. She sat looking thoughtfully out of the window. Very much was passing through her mind. Then Rosalie closed the Bible and, wrapping it carefully in the paper in which it had been kept for so many years, she hid it away in the box again.

It was Sunday evening now, and once more the church bells rang. Once more, the people went past with books in their hands. Rosalie wished she could creep into one of the churches and hear another sermon. But just then her father and the men came back and wanted their tea. Instead of the quiet service, Rosalie had to listen to their loud talking and noisy laughter.

Her father took her to the traveling theater after tea, and made her go through her part of the play again. She was just finishing her rehearsal as the people passed back again from evening service.

CHAPTER 8

Little Mother Manikin

T was Monday night, and Rosalie's mother was dressing to be ready to act in the play. Rosalie was standing beside her, setting out the folds of her mother's white dress, and fetching everything she needed: her large necklace of pearl beads, the wreath of white lilies for her hair, and the bracelets, rings, and other articles of imitation jewelry with which she was adorned. All these Rosalie brought to her, and she put them on one by one, standing before the small looking glass to arrange them.

It was a very thin face which that glass reflected; so ill and careworn, so weary and sad. As soon as she was ready, she sat down on one of the boxes whilst Rosalie dressed herself.

"I'm sure you are not fit to act tonight," said Rosalie.

"Hush!" said her mother. "Don't speak of that now.

Come, sit beside me and let me do your hair for you. And before we go, Rosalie dear, sing your little hymn."

Rosalie tried to sing it. But somehow her voice trembled, and she could not sing very steadily. There was such a sad expression in her mother's face that Rosalie burst into tears and threw her arms round her mother's neck.

"Don't cry, darling, don't cry!" said her mother. "What is the matter with you, Rosalie?"

"Oh, Mother, I don't want you to go tonight!"

"Hush, little one!" said her mother. "I want you to make your mother a promise tonight. I want you to promise me that, if you can ever get away from this life, you will do so. It's not good for you, darling, all this traveling and acting. It makes my heart ache every time you have to go to it. You'll leave it if you can, Rosalie; won't you?"

"Yes, if you'll come with me," said Rosalie.

Her mother shook her head. "No, dear; I shall never leave the caravan now. I chose this life. But you didn't choose it, child. I pray every day that God may save you from it. You remember that village we passed through, where the lady gave you the hymn on the card?"

"Yes, Mother. Where we had the milk and bread."

"Do you remember the house by the church I sent you to look at?"

"Oh, yes, the vicarage with a pretty garden, and a lady and a girl gathering roses."

"That lady was my sister Lucy, Rosalie."

"Aunt Lucy!" said Rosalie. "And was that girl my cousin?"

"Yes, darling. I knew it was your Aunt Lucy as soon as that young woman mentioned her name. Lucy married a minister named Mr. Leslie; and it was just like her to read to those people in the cottages, just as she used to do to me."

"Then I've really seen her?" said Rosalie.

"Yes, darling. And now I want you to promise me that if you ever have the opportunity of getting to your Aunt Lucy without your father knowing it, you'll go. I've written a letter to her, and I've hidden it in this box—inside the case where the locket is. And if you can ever go to your Aunt Lucy, give her the letter. You will, won't you, Rosalie? And show her that locket. She will remember it as soon as she sees it. And tell her, darling, that I never, never parted with it all these long years."

"But why won't you come with me, Mother?"

"Don't ask me that now, darling. It's nearly time for us to go into the theater. But before you go, just read those verses about your picture once more. We shall just have time for it before your father comes."

So Rosalie read the parable of the lost sheep.

"Rosalie," said her mother, when she had finished, "there are four words in that story which I've had in my mind so many times since you read it last."

"What are they, Mother?"

" 'Until he find it,' Rosalie. All last night I lay awake coughing, and I kept thinking there was no hope for me. It was no use my asking the Good Shepherd to look for me. But all of a sudden those words came back to me just as if someone had said them to me. 'Until he find it—until he find it. He goeth after that which is lost until he find it.' It seems He doesn't give up. He goes on looking until He finds it. And then it seemed to me, Rosalie—I don't know if I was right, I don't know if I even dare hope it, but it seemed to me last night that perhaps, if He takes such pains and looks so long—if He goes on until He find it—there might even be a chance for me."

"Are you ready?" called Augustus' voice, at the door of the caravan. "We're just about to start."

Rosalie and her mother jumped up hastily and, thrusting the Bible into the box, they hurried down the caravan steps and went into the theater. There were still a few minutes before the performance commenced. Rosalie made her mother sit down on a chair out of sight at the back of the stage, so she might rest as long as possible.

Several of the company came up and asked Rosalie's mother how she was. Rosalie looked in their faces, and read there that they did not think her mother well enough to work; and it filled her heart with sorrowful concern.

Her mother repeated the words of the play as if they were extremely distasteful to her—as if she could hardly bear the sound of her own voice. She never smiled at the bursts of applause. She repeated her part almost mechanically and, from time to time, Rosalie saw her mother's eyes fill with tears. She crept to her side and put her hand in her mother's as they went up to the platform after the first performance was over.

Her mother's hand was burning with fever, and yet she shivered from head to foot as they went out on the platform into the chill night air.

"Mother," said Rosalie, in a whisper, "you ought to go back to the caravan now."

But Rosalie's mother shook her head.

About half way through the next play there came a long piece which Rosalie had to recite alone, the piece which her father had been teaching her during the last week. She was just half way through it when, suddenly, her eyes fell on her mother, who was standing at the opposite side of the stage.

All the color had gone from her face, and it seemed to Rosalie that each moment her face was growing whiter.

She quite forgot the words she was saying. All remembrance of them faded from her mind and she came to a sudden stop. Her father's promptings were all in vain. She could hear nothing he said—she could see nothing but her mother.

And then her mother fell. Some of the actors carried her from the tent. Rosalie rushed forward to follow her, and the noise in the theater became deafening. But she was stopped on the stairs by her father, who ordered her to return immediately and finish her part.

Rosalie went on with her recital, trembling in every limb. Her mother's place was taken by another actress, and the play went on as before. But Rosalie's heart was not there. It was filled with a terrible, sickening dread. What had become of her mother? Who was with her? Were they taking good care of her?

Then a horrible fear came over her lest her mother should be dead—lest she should never hear her mother speak again.

As soon as the play was over, she went up to her father. In spite of the annoyed expression of his face, she begged him to allow her to leave the theater and go to her mother. He told her angrily that she had spoilt his profits quite enough for one night, and she must take care to dare not do so again. She must stay until the theater closed for the night!

What a long time that seemed to Rosalie. When they went out on the platform between the performances, she gazed anxiously in the direction of her mother's caravan. A light was burning inside, but more than that Rosalie could not see.

It seemed as if the long hours would never pass away. Each time she went through her recital she felt glad she had one less time to say it. Each time that the town-hall clock struck she counted the hours before the theater would close. And yet, when all was over, and when Rosalie was allowed to return to the caravan, she hardly dared to enter.

Very, very gently she opened the door. There was a candle burning on the table, and by its light Rosalie could see her mother lying on the bed. She was very pale, and her eyes were tightly closed. But she was breathing, she was not dead. The relief was so great that Rosalie burst into tears.

When she first came into the caravan she thought that her mother was alone, but a small hoarse whisper came from the corner of the caravan. "Don't be frightened, my dear!" it said. "Toby told me about your mother, and so I came to sit with her till you arrived."

Rosalie walked to her mother's side, and on the box by the bed she found a little old lady about three feet high, with a very wrinkled face.

"Who are you?" asked Rosalie in surprise.

"I belong to the dwarf show, my dear," said the old woman. "There are four of us there, and not one of us is more than three feet high."

"But isn't the show on tonight?" asked Rosalie.

"Yes, it's going on, my dear; it always goes on," said the tiny woman. "But I'm old and ugly, you see, so I can be better spared than the others. I only go in sometimes, my dear. Old age must have its liberties, you see."

"Thank you so much for taking care of my mother," said Rosalie. "Has she spoken to you yet?"

"Yes, my dear," said the old woman; "she spoke once. But I couldn't hear what she said well. I tried to climb up near her to listen. But, you see, I'm only three feet high, so I couldn't quite manage it. I thought it was something about a sheep, but of course it couldn't be that, my dear. There are no sheep here!"

"Oh yes!" said Rosalie. "That would be it. We had been reading about sheep before we went into the theater."

Just then there was a noise at the door of the caravan, and Augustus entered. He went up to his wife, and felt her pulse. Then he muttered, "She's all right now; let her have a good sleep, that's all she wants, Rosalie."

He glanced at the dwarf, and then left the caravan and shut the door.

"Rosalie," said the tiny, old woman when he had gone, "I'll stop with you tonight, if you like."

"Oh! would you?" said Rosalie; "I should be so glad."

She felt as if she could not bear all those long, dark hours alone with her mother.

"Yes," said the dwarf; "I'll stay. Only you must go and tell them in our tent. Can you find it, do you think?"

"Where is it?" said Rosalie.

The woman described the way to her tent and, putting a shawl over her head, Rosalie went in search of it. There were some stalls still lighted up, and the flaring naphtha showed Rosalie an immense picture representing a number of miniature men and women. Above the picture there was a board, on which was written in large letters, "The Royal Show of Dwarfs."

Rosalie had some difficulty in finding the entrance to this large show tent. She felt round it several times, pulling at the canvas in different places, but all to no purpose. Then she heard voices inside, laughing and talking. Going as near to these as possible, she put her mouth to a hole in the canvas, and called out, "Please, will you let me in? I've brought a message from the little lady that lives here."

There was a great shuffling in the tent after this, and a clinking and chinking of money. Then a piece of the canvas was pulled aside, and a squeaky little voice called out, "Come in, whoever you are, and let us hear what you've got to say."

So Rosalie crept in through the canvas, and stepped into the middle of the tent.

It was a strange scene which she saw when she looked round. Three dwarfs stood before her, dressed in the most extraordinary costumes, and far above over their heads there towered a tall and very thin giant. On the floor were scattered tiny tables, chairs, and dolls' umbrellas, which they had been using in their performance.

"What is it, my dear?" asked the giant loftily, as Rosalie entered.

"Please," said Rosalie, "I've brought a message from the little lady that belongs to this show."

"Mother Manikin," said one of the dwarfs, in an explanatory tone.

"Yes, Mother Manikin," repeated the giant; and the two other dwarfs nodded their heads in assent.

"My mother's very ill," said Rosalie, "and she's taking care of her, and she's going to stay all night and I was to tell you."

"All right," said the giant, majestically.

"All right," echoed the three dwarfs.

Then the two lady dwarfs seized Rosalie by the hand and wanted her to sit down and have supper with them. But Rosalie shook her head and explained that she must not leave her mother nor Mother Manikin.

"Quite right," said the giant, in a superior voice.

"Quite right, child."

"Quite right, child, quite right," repeated the three dwarfs.

Then they escorted Rosalie to the door of the show, and bowed her gracefully out.

"Tell Mother Manikin not to come home in daylight," called the giant, as Rosalie was disappearing through the canvas.

"No, no," said the three dwarfs. "Not in daylight!"

"Why not?" said Rosalie.

"Our pennies," said the giant, mysteriously.

"Yes, our pennies and halfpennies for seeing the show," repeated the dwarfs. "We must not make ourselves too cheap."

"Good night, child," said the giant.

"Good night, child," said the dwarfs.

Although she was sad, they almost made Rosalie smile. They were such tiny people to call her "child" in that superior manner. She hurried back to the caravan and, after telling Mother Manikin she had given the message to her friends, she sat by her mother's side.

It was a great comfort having Mother Manikin there. She was so kind and considerate, so thoughtful and clever. She always seemed to know exactly what was wanted; though Rosalie's mother was too weak to ask for anything.

All night long her mother lay still, sometimes entirely unconscious, at other times opening her eyes and trying to smile at Rosalie, who was now sitting at the foot of the bed. Mother Manikin did everything that had to be done. She was evidently accustomed to a sickroom, and knew the best way of making those she nursed comfortable. She climbed on a chair and arranged the pillows so that the sick woman could breathe more easily. And, after a time, she made the poor, tired girl lie down at the foot of the bed, wrapped in a woollen shawl. In a few minutes Rosalie fell asleep.

When she awoke, the grey light was stealing in at the caravan window. She raised herself on the bed and looked round. At first she thought she was dreaming, but presently the recollection of the night before came back to her. There was her mother sleeping quietly on the bed, and there was little Mother Manikin sitting on the old box, never having allowed herself to sleep all the long night.

"Oh, Mother Manikin," said Rosalie, getting down from the bed and throwing her arms round the little, old woman's neck. "How good you are!"

"Hush, child!" said the dwarf. "Don't wake your mother. She's sleeping so peacefully now, and has been for the last hour."

"I'm so glad!" said Rosalie. "Do you think she will soon be better, Mother Manikin?"

"I can't say, my dear. Tell me what that picture is about up there. I've been looking at it all night."

"Oh, that's *my* picture," said Rosalie proudly. "The shepherd has been looking everywhere for that lamb. At last He has found it, and carried it home on His shoulder. He is so glad it is found, and now He is holding it to keep it safe in His arms."

"And what is that writing underneath?" asked the old woman. "I can't read, my dear, you see; I am so scholar."

" 'Rejoice with me; for I have found my sheep which was lost. There is joy in the presence of the angels of God over one sinner that repenteth.' "

"What does that mean, child?" asked the old woman.

"I think it means Jesus is like a shepherd, and He is

looking for us, Mother Manikin. It makes Him so glad when He finds us."

The dwarf nodded her head in assent.

"We ask Him every day to find us, Mother Manikin—Mother and me. And the story says He will look for us until He finds us. Shall I read it to you? It's what Mother and I were reading before we went into the play."

Rosalie went to the box and brought out the black Bible. Then, sitting at Mother Manikin's feet, she read her favorite story of the lost sheep.

"Has He found *you,* Mother Manikin?" Rosalie said, as she closed the book.

The dwarf put her head on one side, and smoothed her tiny, grey curls, but made no answer. Rosalie was almost afraid she had upset her, and did not like to say anything more. A long time afterwards—so long that Rosalie had been thinking of a dozen things since—Mother Manikin answered her question, and said in a strange whisper: "No, child; he *hasn't* found *me.*"

"Won't you ask Him, Mother Manikin?" said Rosalie simply.

"Yes, child; I'll begin today," replied the dwarf. "I'll begin now, if you'll say the words for me."

Rosalie slipped from her stool and, kneeling on the floor of the caravan, she said aloud: "Good Shepherd, you are looking for Mother and for me; please look for Mother Manikin too. And please put her on your shoulder and carry her home. Amen."

"Amen!" said old Mother Manikin, in her hoarse whisper.

She did not talk any more after this. About six o'clock there came a rap on the caravan door, and a woman in a long

66

cloak appeared, asking if Mother Manikin were there. She belonged to the Royal Show of Dwarfs, and she had come to take Mother Manikin home before the business of the marketplace commenced. Some men were already passing by on their way to work; so the woman wrapped Mother Manikin in a shawl, and carried her home like a baby, covering her with her cloak so that no one should see who she was.

Rosalie realized this was what the others had meant when they said they must not make themselves too cheap. People would not pay to see dwarfs if they could see them walking in the fairground.

Rosalie thanked Mother Manikin with tears in her eyes for all her kindness; and the little woman promised to come again soon and see how her patient was.

CHAPTER 9

The Doctor's Visit

ROSALIE was not alone for long after Mother Manikin left her. There was a rap at the door, and on opening it she found Toby.

"Miss Rosie," he said, "how is she now?"

"I think she is sleeping quietly, Toby," said Rosalie.

"I would have come before, but I was afraid of disturbing her," said Toby. "I've been thinking of her all night; I didn't get many winks of sleep, Miss Rosie!"

"Oh! Toby, was it you that fetched little Mother Manikin?"

"Yes, Miss Rosie. I used to belong to their show before I came to Master. And once, when I had a fever, Mother Manikin nursed me all the time I had it. So I was sure she would know what to do."

"She *is* a kind, little thing!" said Rosalie.

"Yes, missie; she may only have a little body, but there's a great, kind heart inside it. But, Miss Rosie, I wanted to tell you something. I'm going to fetch a doctor to see missis."

"Oh, Toby! but what will my father say?"

"It's he that has sent me, Miss Rosie. You see, I think he's ashamed. You should have seen the men last night, when they were shutting up the theater after you had gone away. They went up to Master and gave him a bit of their minds about letting missis come on the stage when she was so ill. They told him it was a sin and a shame the way he treated her, taking less care of her than if she were one of his old horses. Not that he's over and above good to them neither.

"Well, Master didn't like it, Miss Rosie, and he was very angry at the time. But this morning, as soon as it was light, he told me to get up and fetch a doctor to see missis at once. So I thought I'd better tell you, Miss Rosie, that you might put things straight before he comes."

As soon as Toby had gone, Rosalie put the caravan in order, and anxiously awaited the doctor's arrival. Her father brought him in, and stayed there in the caravan whilst the doctor felt the sick woman's pulse, and asked Rosalie several questions about the cough. Then they went out together, leaving Rosalie. She had not dared to ask the doctor what he thought of her mother while her father was present, and her heart was full of anxious fear.

Augustus came in soon after the doctor left, and Rosalie crept up to him and asked what he had said of her mother.

"He says she is very ill," said her father shortly, in a voice which told Rosalie that she must ask no more questions. Then he sat down beside the bed for about half an hour and looked more gentle than Rosalie had ever seen him before.

She was sure the doctor must have told him that her mother was dying.

Rosalie's father did not speak. There was no sound in the caravan but the ticking of the clock which was fastened to a nail in the corner, and the occasional falling of the cinders in the ashpan of the iron stove. Augustus' recollections were not pleasant as he sat by his wife's bed.

All his cruel treatment came back to his mind—the hard words he had spoken to her, the unkind things he had said of her and, above all, the hard-hearted way in which he had made her come on the stage the night before, when she was almost too ill to stand.

He suddenly jumped up and went out without saying a word to his daughter, slammed the door and walked to the marketplace where he met some of his friends.

That evening Rosalie was made to act in the play. Her father insisted on it. It was impossible for him to spare her, he said, and to fill up both her place *and* her mother's also. Rosalie begged him in vain to excuse her. So, with an aching heart, she went to the Royal Show of Dwarfs and asked for Mother Manikin.

The good, little woman was indignant when Rosalie told her she was not allowed to stay with her mother. She promised to come immediately and sit beside the sick woman. The other dwarfs rather grumbled at this arrangement. But Mother Manikin shook her little fist at them and called them hard-hearted creatures, and declared once more that old age must have its liberties!

"Oh! Mother Manikin," said Rosalie, "and you had no sleep last night!"

"Oh! my dear, I'm all right," said the little woman. "I had a nap this morning. Don't trouble about me; and Miss Mab and Master Puck ought to be ashamed of themselves for wanting me when there's that poor woman so ill out there. Bless me, my dears!" said Mother Manikin turning to the dwarfs, "what should you want with an ugly little thing like me? It's you lovely young creatures that the crowds come to see. So I'll wish you good night, my dears. Take care of yourselves, and don't get into any mischief while I'm away! Where's Susannah?"

"Here, ma'am," said the woman who had come for Mother Manikin that morning.

"Carry me to Joyce's van," said the little old woman, jumping on a chair and holding out her arms.

Susannah wrapped her in a cloak, and took her quickly in the direction of the theater, Rosalie walking by her side.

Then the little woman helped Rosalie to dress for the play, pulling out the folds of her white dress for her, and combing her long hair in a most motherly fashion. When Rosalie was ready she stood looking thoughtfully at her mother's pale face. But as she was looking, her mother's eyes opened, and gazed tenderly at her. Then, to the girl's joy, her mother spoke.

"Rosalie," she whispered, "I feel better tonight. Kiss your mother, Rosie."

Rosalie bent down and kissed her mother's face, and her long, dark hair lay across her mother's pillow.

"Who is this, taking care of me, Rosalie?"

"It's a little lady Toby knows, Mother. She's ever so kind, and she says she will sit with you all the time I'm out. I didn't want to leave you. I wanted so much to stay, but I cannot be spared, father says."

"Never mind," said her mother. "I feel a little better tonight. I should like a cup of tea."

71

Mother Manikin had a cup of tea ready almost at once. She was the quickest little person Rosalie had ever seen; yet she was so quiet that her quick movements did not in the least disturb the sick woman.

"How kind you are!" said Rosalie's mother, as the dwarf climbed on a chair to give her the tea.

"There's nothing like tea," said the tiny woman, nodding her wise head. "Give me a cup of tea, and I don't care what I go without! You're better tonight, ma'am."

"Yes," said Rosalie's mother. "I can talk a little now. I heard a great deal you said last night, though I could not speak to you. I heard you talking about Rosalie's picture."

"Well, fancy that!" said the little woman, cheerily. "To think of that, Rosalie! Why, she heard us talking. Bless me, child, she's not so ill after all!"

"I think that did me good," said Rosalie's mother. "I heard Rosalie pray."

"Yes," said Mother Manikin. "She put me in her prayer, bless her! I haven't forgotten that!"

Rosalie's mother seemed very tired now, and the dwarf would not let her talk any more, but made her lie quietly without moving. When Rosalie left her to go on the stage she was sleeping peacefully, with Mother Manikin sitting by her side. When Rosalie returned late that night, there she was, sitting still. And she insisted on Rosalie creeping into bed beside her mother so that she might have a proper night's rest, for there was only the one, small bed in the caravan. Rosalie was completely exhausted. The worry and the hard work had made her very tired.

The next day, Rosalie's mother was able to take some food, and to talk in whispers from time to time.

"Rosalie," she said, that afternoon, "there is a verse come

back to me which our old nurse taught me. I haven't thought of it for years, but that night when I was so ill I woke saying it."

"What is it?" asked Rosalie.

" 'All we like sheep have gone astray; we have turned every one to his own way; and the Lord hath laid on Him the iniquity of us all.' That was it, dear. I remember it so clearly now."

"Mother Manikin told me you said something about sheep," said Rosalie.

"Yes, that was it," said Rosalie's mother, almost to herself. "It's such a beautiful verse. 'All we like sheep have gone astray'; that's just like me. I've gone astray, oh! so far astray. And 'have turned every one to his own way.' That's me again—my own way, that's just what it was. I chose it myself. I *would* have my own way. It's just like me, Rosalie!"

"And what's the end of the verse, Mother."

" 'The Lord hath laid on Him the iniquity of us all.' That means Jesus. The Lord put all our sins on Jesus when He died on the cross."

"Did God put *your* sins on Jesus," asked Rosalie.

"Yes, child; I think it *must* mean mine, because it says, 'the iniquity of us *all.*' I think 'all' must take me in, Rosalie. I have been asking Him to let it mean me because, you know, if the sin is laid on *Him*, Rosie darling, *I* shan't have to bear it too."

The woman lay back quietly when she had said this. Rosalie brought her some beef tea which Mother Manikin had made for her, and which was simmering on the iron stove.

The little woman came back one more night to stay with Rosalie's mother whilst the play was going on. The theater

73

closed earlier that night, for a large fair was to be held at a town some way off. Augustus Joyce was very anxious to be present there. Since he did not think there was much more money to be made in Lesborough, he determined to start at once. So the moment that the last person had left the theater, Augustus and his men hastily took off the clothes in which they had been acting, slipped on their working coats, and began to pull down the scenery.

All night long they were hammering and knocking down and packing up, and when morning dawned they were ready to start. And so were many other shows from the fair.

"Miss Rosie," said Toby's voice, at about five o'clock that morning, "they are going except us. Master says *we* can wait a bit longer, to give missis a little more rest. He and the other men are leaving at once, to set up the theater and get everything ready. Master says it will be time enough if we are there by the first night of the fair. He can do without you until then, he says."

"I am very glad my mother hasn't to be moved just yet," said Rosalie. "The shaking would be bad for her, I'm sure."

Augustus came into the caravan for a few minutes before he set off. He told Rosalie that they could stay for two days longer; but on Saturday morning they must be off early, so as to get into the town by Sunday night.

"I wouldn't have you away from the play there, Rosalie, not for the world. It's a large seaside town, and I hope to make a pretty penny, if everyone pulls his weight."

"Augustus," said his wife, quietly, "can you stay five minutes with me before you go?"

"Well," said Augustus, taking out his watch, "perhaps I might spare five minutes. But you must be quick. I ought to be off by now."

"Rosalie darling," said her mother, "leave me and your father alone."

Rosalie went down the steps of the caravan, shutting the door gently behind her. She stood watching her father's men, who were yoking the horses in the wagons and tying ropes round the different loads, to prevent anything falling off.

As soon as she was gone, her mother laid her hand on her husband's arm, and said, "Augustus, there are two things I want to ask you."

"What are they?" said the man, shortly, crossing his legs and leaning back on his chair.

"The first is, Augustus, that you will find a home for Rosalie when I die. Don't take her about from fair to fair. She will have no mother to take care of her and I can't bear to think of her being left here all alone."

"All alone!" said Augustus angrily. "She will have *me!* She will be all right if *I'm* here! I'm not going to let the child go, just when she's beginning to be useful. Besides, where would you have her go?"

Rosalie's mother did not tell the secret hope which was in her heart.

"I thought," she said, "you might find some motherly person out in the country somewhere, who would take care of her for very little money, and would send her to school and see she was brought up properly."

"Oh, nonsense!" said Augustus. "She will be all right with me, and I'm not going to lose a pretty child like that from the stage! Why, half the people come to see the 'lovely little actress,' as they call her. Well, the five minutes are up," said Augustus, looking at his watch; "I must be off."

"There was something else I wanted to ask you, Augustus."

"Well, what is it? Be quick!"

"I wanted to tell you that the last fortnight I have been feeling that, when one comes to die, there is nothing worthwhile in this world except to know that your soul is safe. I've led a bad life, Augustus. I've often been disagreeable to you. But all I want now is that the Good Shepherd should seek me and find me, before it is too late."

"Is that *all?*" said her husband, putting on his coat.

"No, Augustus. I wanted to ask you something. Are *you* ready to die?"

"There's time enough to think of that," said her husband with a laugh.

Yet there was an uneasy expression in his face as he said it, which showed that the question was not one he wanted to face.

"Oh, Augustus! You don't know how long there may be," said his wife, in tears now.

"Well," said he, "if life's so short, we must get all the play we can out of it!"

"But what of the other life, Augustus—the long life that's coming?"

"Oh! that may take care of itself," said her husband, scornfully, as he lighted his pipe at the stove. Then, wishing his wife a pleasant journey, he went down the steps of the caravan and closed the door.

His wife turned over on her pillow and wept. She had made a very great effort in speaking to her husband, and it had been no use at all.

A few minutes afterwards the other wagons rumbled past, as the theater party set off on their journey. Rosalie and her mother were left behind with their caravan, to watch the rest of the fair people prepare to leave.

CHAPTER 10

Britannia

LL day long the packing went on, and one by one the shows moved off. The market-place became more and more empty.

In the afternoon Toby came to the caravan to inform Rosalie that the Royal Show of Dwarfs was just going to start, and Mother Manikin wanted to say goodbye to her.

"Mind you thank her, Rosalie," said the sick woman, "and give her my love."

"Yes, Mother," said the girl, "I won't forget."

She found the four dwarfs sitting in a tiny covered wagon, in which they were to take their journey. Rosalie was cautiously admitted, and the door closed carefully after her. Mother Manikin said goodbye with tears in her eyes. They were not going to the same fair as Rosalie's father, and she did not know when they would meet again. She gave Rosalie very detailed directions about the beef tea, and slipped a tiny parcel in her pocket. She told her to give it to her mother.

And then she whispered in Rosalie's ear, "I haven't forgotten to ask the Good Shepherd to find me, child; and don't you leave me out, my dear, when you say your prayers at night."

"Come, Mother Manikin," said Master Puck, "we must be off!"

Mother Manikin shook her fist at him, saying, "Old age must have its liberties!" This seemed to be a favorite saying of hers.

Then she put her little arms round Rosalie's neck and kissed her. As soon as Rosalie had gone, the signal was given for their departure, and the Royal Show of Dwarfs left the marketplace.

Rosalie ran back to her mother and gave her Mother Manikin's parcel. It was wrapped in several layers of paper, which Rosalie took off one by one. Then came an envelope, inside which was a coin. She took it out and held it up to her mother; it was a half-sovereign!

Mother Manikin had taken that half-sovereign from her small bag of savings, and she had put it in that envelope with even a gladder heart than Rosalie's mother had when she received it!

"Oh, Rosalie," said the sick woman, "I can afford to have some more beef tea now!"

And it was not only at her evening prayer that Rosalie mentioned Mother Manikin's name that day. Right now she knelt down to ask the Good Shepherd to seek and to save little Mother Mankikin. Then Rosalie sat by her mother's side, watching her tenderly and carefully, and trying to be like Mother Manikin in the way she arranged her pillows and cared for her.

Rosalie felt very lonely the next day. Toby had slept in an inn in the town. The marketplace was empty, and no one came near the one solitary caravan—no one except an officer of the board of health to inquire what was the cause of delay, and whether the sick woman was suffering from any infectious complaint.

People passed the marketplace and went to the various shops, but no one else came near Rosalie and her mother.

The sick woman slept the greater part of the day, and spoke very little. Every now and then Rosalie heard her repeat to herself the last verse of the hymn on the card.

> "Lord, I come without delaying;
> To thine arms at once I flee,
> Lest no more I hear Thee saying,
> 'Come, come to Me.' "

Then night came, and Rosalie sat by her mother's side. She did not like to go to sleep, in case her mother should awake and want something. The town-hall clock struck, but it was the only sound that broke the stillness.

Rosalie kept an oil lamp burning and every now and then she put some wood in the iron stove so that the beef tea would be ready whenever her mother wanted it. Many times she gazed at her picture, and wished *she* were the lamb safe in the Good Shepherd's arms.

The next morning, Rosalie herad Toby's voice as soon as it was light.

"Miss Rosie," he said, "can I come in for a minute?"

Rosalie opened the door, and Toby was much distressed to see how tired she looked.

"You mustn't make yourself ill, Miss Rosie. You really mustn't!" he said, reproachfully.

"I'll try not, Toby," Rosalie said. "Perhaps the country air will do me good."

"Yes, missie, maybe it will. I think we'd better start at once, because I don't want to have to go fast. The slower we go the better it will be for missis. And we will stop somewhere for the night. If we come to a village we can stop there, and I'll find some barn to creep into, or if there's no barn, there's sure to be a haystack. I've slept on a haystack before this, Miss Rosie!"

In about half an hour Toby had everything ready, and they left the marketplace. Very slowly and carefully he drove; yet even so, the shaking was bad for Rosalie's mother.

Rosalie opened the caravan door, and every now and then spoke to Toby. He did not whistle today, nor call out to his horse, but seemed very thoughtful and quiet.

"What do you think of stopping here for the night, Miss Rosie?" asked Toby towards evening.

They had come to a very quiet place on the edge of a large moor. A great pine forest stretched on one side of them, and the trees looked dark and solemn in the fading light. At the edge of this wood was a stone wall, against which Toby drew up the caravan, so that it would be sheltered from the wind.

On the other side of the road was the moor, stretching on for miles and miles. In a little sheltered corner, surrounded by furze bushes, Toby said he would sleep.

"I shall be close by, Miss Rosie," he said. "I sleep pretty sound; but if only you call out 'Toby' I shall be at your side in a twinkling. I always wake in a trice when I hear my name

On the moor.

called. You won't be frightened out here, Miss Rosie, will you?"

"No," said Rosalie, "I think not."

But she gazed rather anxiously down the road. The trees were throwing dark shadows across the path, and their branches were waving gloomily in the evening breeze. Rosalie shivered as she looked round at the dark forest behind her.

"I'll tell you what, Miss Rosie," said Toby, as he finished eating his supper. "I'll sit on the steps of the caravan, if you are frightened at all. No, no; never you mind me; I shall be all right. One night's sitting up won't hurt me!"

But Rosalie would not allow it. She insisted Toby lie down comfortably to sleep on the soft heather, and made him take a warm shawl, that he might wrap himself in it, for it was a very cold night. Then she carefully bolted the caravan door, closed the windows, and crept to her sleeping mother's side. She sat on the bed, put her head on the pillow, and tried to sleep also. But the intense stillness made her head ache, for she kept sitting up in the bed to listen, and to strain her ears—longing for any sound to break the silence.

Yet when a sound *did* come—when the wind swept over the trees, and made the branches which hung over the caravan creak as they swayed to and fro—Rosalie became filled with fear. The lack of sleep that last few nights was telling on her, and had made her nervous and sensitive. At last she found the matches and lit the lamp, that she would not feel quite so lonely.

She took her Bible from the box and began to read. As she read, Rosalie no longer felt alone. She had a wonderful realization of the Good Shepherd's presence, and a feeling that her prayer was heard, and that He was indeed holding her in His strong arms.

If it had not been for this, she would have screamed out loud when, about an hour afterwards, there came a tap at the caravan door. Rosalie jumped from her seat and peeped out between the muslin curtains. She could just see a dark figure on the caravan steps.

"Is it you, Toby?" she asked, opening the window cautiously.

"No, it's me," said a girl's voice. "Have you got a fire in there?"

"Who are you?" said Rosalie, trying to sound brave.

"I'll tell you when I get in," said the girl. "Let me come and warm myself by your fire!"

Rosalie did not know what to do. She did not much like opening the door, for how could she tell who this stranger was? She almost called to Toby, when the sound of crying made her change her mind.

"What's the matter?" Rosalie asked.

"I'm cold and hungry and miserable!" the girl said, with a sob. "I saw your light, and I thought you would let me in."

Rosalie hesitated no longer. She unbolted the door, and the dark figure on the steps came in. She threw off a long cloak with which she was covered; and Rosalie could see that she was about sixteen or seventeen years old. She had been crying and her eyes were swollen and red. She was as cold as ice; there seemed to be no feeling in her hands, and her teeth chattered as she sat down on the bench by the side of the stove.

Rosalie put some tea into a little pan and made it hot. And when the girl had drunk this she seemed better, and more inclined to talk.

"Is that your mother?" she said, glancing at the bed where

Rosalie's mother was sleeping.

"Yes," said Rosalie, in a whisper. "We mustn't wake her. She is very, very ill. The doctor has given her some medicine to make her sleep whilst we're traveling."

"I have a mother," said the girl.

"Have you?" said Rosalie. "Where is she?"

But the girl did not answer this question. She buried her face in her hands and began to cry again.

"I wish you would tell me what's the matter," Rosalie said. "Who are you?"

"I'm Britannia," said the girl, without looking up.

"Britannia?" repeated Rosalie, in a puzzled voice. "What do you mean?"

"You were at Lesborough, weren't you?" said the girl.

"Yes, we've just come from Lesborough."

"Then didn't you see the circus there?"

"Oh, yes," said Rosalie. "The procession passed us on the road as we were going into the town."

"Well, I'm Britannia," said the girl. "Didn't you see me on the top of the last carriage? I had a white dress on and a scarlet scarf."

"Yes," said Rosalie, "I remember. You had a great fork in your hand."

"Yes; they call it a trident, and they called me Britannia."

"But what are you doing *here?*" asked Rosalie.

"I've run away; I couldn't stand it any longer. I'm going home."

"Where *is* your home?"

"Oh, a long way off. I don't suppose I shall ever get there. I haven't a penny in my pocket, and I'm tired out already. I've been walking all night—and all day."

Then she began to cry again, so loudly that Rosalie was

afraid she would awake and alarm her mother.

"Oh, Britannia!" she said. "Don't cry! Tell me what's the matter?"

"Call me by my own name," said the girl, with another sob. "I'm not Britannia now, I'm Jessie. 'Little Jess,' my mother always calls me."

And at the mention of her mother she cried again as if her heart would break.

"Jessie," said Rosalie, laying her hand on her arm, "won't you tell me about it?"

The girl stopped crying, and as soon as she was calmer she told Rosalie her story.

"I've got such a lovely mother; it's that which made me cry," she said.

"Your mother isn't in the circus, then, is she?" said Rosalie.

"Oh no," said the girl; and she almost smiled through her tears. "You don't know my mother or you wouldn't ask that! No, she lives in a village a long way from here. I'm going to her; at least I *think* I am; I don't know if I dare."

"Why not?" asked Rosalie. "Are you frightened of your mother?"

"No, I'm not frightened of her," said the girl. "But I'm almost ashamed to go back. She doesn't know where I am now. I expect she has had no sleep since I ran away."

"When did you run away?" asked Rosalie quietly.

"It will be three weeks ago now," said Jessie. "But it seems more like three months. I never was so miserable in all my life before. I've cried myself to sleep every night."

"Whatever made you leave your mother?"

"It was that circus. It came to the next town to where we lived. All the girls in the village were going to it, and I wanted to go with them. But my mother wouldn't let me."

"Then how did you see it?" asked Rosalie.

"I didn't see it that day. The girls told me all about it, and what a fine procession it was, and how the ladies were dressed in silver and gold, and the men in shining armor. I almost cried with disappointment because I had not seen it, too. The girls said it would only be in the town one more day, and then it was going away. When I got into bed that night I made up my mind I would go and have a look at it the next day."

"But did your mother let you?" asked Rosalie.

"No. I knew it was no use asking her. I meant to slip out of the house before she knew anything about it. But it so happened that she was called away to the next village to see my aunt, who was ill."

"And did you go when she was out?"

"Yes, I did," said Jessie. "And I told her a lie about it."

"What did you say?"

"She said to me before she went, 'Little Jess, you'll take care of Maggie and baby, won't you, dear? You'll not let any harm come to them?' And I said, 'No, mother, I won't.' But as I said it my cheeks turned hot, and I felt as if my mother must see how they were burning. But she did not seem to notice. She turned back and kissed me, and kissed little Maggie and the baby, and then she went to my aunt's, saying she would be back by tea time. I watched her until she was out of sight, and then I put on my best clothes and set off for the town."

"And what did you do with Maggie and the baby?" asked Rosalie. "Did you take them with you?"

"No. That's the worst of it," said the girl. "I left them. I put the baby in his crib upstairs, and I told Maggie to look after him. Then I put the guard in front of the fire and locked them in. I put the key under the mat of the front door. I thought I should only be away a short time."

"How long were you?"

"When I got to the town the procession was just passing, and I stopped to look at it. And when I saw the men and women sitting up on the carriages, I thought they were kings and queens. Well, I went to the circus and saw all that was to be seen. Then I looked at the church clock, and found it was five o'clock. I knew my mother would be home, and I did not like to go back. I wondered what she would say to me about leaving the children. So I walked round the circus for some time looking at the gilded carriages which were drawn up in the field. And as I was looking at them an old man came up and began talking to me. He asked me what I thought of the circus. I told him I thought it was splendid. Then he asked me what I liked best, and I said those ladies in gold and silver who were sitting on the gilt carriages.

" 'Would you like to be dressed like that?' he asked me.

" 'Yes, I would,' I said, as I looked down at my dress—my best Sunday dress, which I had once thought so smart.

" 'Well,' he said, mysteriously, 'I don't know, but perhaps I may get you that chance. Just wait here a minute, and I'll see.'

"I stood there half afraid, hardly knowing what to wish. At last he came back, and told me to follow him. He took me into a room, and there I found a very grand lady—at least she looked like one. She asked me if I would like to come and be Britannia in the circus and ride on the gilt carriage."

"And what did you say?" asked Rosalie.

"I thought it was a great chance for me, and I told her I would stay. I was so excited about it that I hardly knew where I was. It seemed just as if someone was asking me to be a queen. And it was not till I got into bed that I let myself think of my mother."

"Did you think of her then?" asked Rosalie.

"Yes. I couldn't help thinking of her then. But there were six or seven other girls in the room, and I was afraid of them hearing me cry, so I hid my face under the bedclothes. The next day we moved from that town, and I felt miserable all the time we were traveling. Then the circus was set up again, and we went in the procession."

"Did you like that?" asked Rosalie.

"No. It was not as nice as I expected. It was a cold day, and the white dress was very thin, and oh! I was so dizzy on that carriage. It was such a height, and I felt every moment as if I should fall. And they were so unkind to me. I was miserable because I kept thinking of my mother; and when they were talking and laughing I used to cry, and they didn't like that. They said I was very different than the last girl they had. She had left them to be married, and they were looking for a fresh girl when they met me.

"They thought I had a pretty face and would do very well. But they were angry with me for looking so miserable, and found more and more fault with me. They were always quarreling. Long after we went to bed they were shouting at each other. I got so tired of it; I *did* wish I had never left home. And then we came to Lesborough, and at last I could bear it no longer. I kept dreaming about my home, and when I woke in the night I thought I heard my mother's voice. I made up my mind to run away. I knew they would be very angry; but no money could make me put up with that sort of life. I was thoroughly sick of it.

"And now I'm going home. I ran away the night they left

Lesborough. I got out of the caravan when they were all asleep. I've been walking ever since. I brought a little food with me; but it's all gone now, and how I shall get home I don't know!"

"Poor Jessie!" said Rosalie when the story was told.

"I don't know what my mother will say when I get there," added Jessie.

"She will be *glad* to get you back," said Rosalie. "I don't know what my mother would do if *I* ran away."

"Oh dear!" said Jessie, not really listening. "I hope no harm came to those children. I do hope they are safe. I've thought about that so often."

Then the poor girl seemed very tired and, lying against the wall, she fell asleep whilst Rosalie rested once more against her mother's pillow. Again there was no sound to be heard but the wind sweeping among the dark fir trees. Rosalie was glad to have Jessie there; the place did not seem quite so frightening.

At last her eyes closed, and she forgot her troubles in a refreshing sleep.

CHAPTER 11

The Dream

ROSALIE woke to find her mother watching her.
The early morning light was stealing into
the caravan. Jessie was still asleep in the
corner, with her head leaning against the
wall.

"Rosalie," whispered her mother, "where
are we, and who is that girl?"

"We're half way to the next fair—out on
a moor; and that's Britannia!"

"What do you mean?"

"It's the girl we saw riding on that gilt carriage in
Lesborough. She has run away; she was so miserable there."

Rosalie told the story she had just heard.

"Poor thing! Poor young thing!" said the sick woman.
"I'm glad you asked her in. Mind you give her a good
breakfast. She does well to go back to her mother. It's the

best thing she can do. Do you think it would wake her if you were to sing to me?"

"No, Mother, I shouldn't think so, if I didn't sing very loud."

"Then could you sing me your hymn once more? I've had the tune in my ears all night, and I should so much like to hear the words of it."

So Rosalie sang her hymn. She had a sweet, low voice, and she sang in tune.

> Jesus, I thy face am seeking,
>   Early will I turn to Thee:
> Words of love Thy voice is speaking;
>   "Come, come to Me.
>
> " 'Come to Me when life is dawning,
>   I thy dearest Friend would be;
> In the sunshine of the morning,
>   Come, come to Me.
>
> "Come to Me—oh! do believe Me,
>   I have shed My blood for thee;
> I am waiting to receive thee,
>   Come, come to Me."
>
> Lord, I come without delaying,
>   To thine arms at once I flee,
> Lest no more I hear Thee saying,
>   "Come, come to Me."

When she had finished singing, Jessie opened her eyes, and looked up with a smile, as if she were in the midst of a pleasant dream. Then, as she saw the inside of the caravan, the sick woman, and Rosalie, she remembered where she was, and burst into tears.

"What's the matter?" asked Rosalie.

The Dream

"I was dreaming," replied Jessie.

"Ask her what she was dreaming," said Rosalie's mother.

"I was dreaming I was at home, and it was Sunday, and we were at Bible class, and singing a hymn. I was singing it when I woke, and it made me cry to think it wasn't true."

"Perhaps it was my singing that made you dream it," said Rosalie. "I've been singing to my mother."

"What did you sing?" asked Jessie. "Will you sing it to *me?*"

Rosalie sang the first verse of the hymn again. To her surprise, Jessie jumped up and seized her by the hand.

"Where did you hear *that?*" she asked, hurriedly. "That's the very hymn I was singing in my dream. We sing it on Sunday afternoons in our Bible class."

"I have it on a card," said Rosalie, bringing it down from the wall.

"Why, who gave you that?" said the girl. "It's just like mine! Mine has a ribbon on it just that color! Where *did* you get it?"

"We were passing through a village," said Rosalie, "and a woman gave it to me. We stopped there, and she was singing it outside her cottage door."

"Why, it must have been our village, surely!" said Jessie. "I don't think they have those cards anywhere else! What was the woman like?"

"She was a young woman with a very friendly face. She had a little boy about two years old, and he was playing with his ball in front of the house. His mother was so good to us—she gave us some bread and milk."

"Why, it must have been Mrs. Barker!" said the girl. "She lives close to us. Our cottage is just a little farther up the road. To think that you've been to our village! Oh! I wish you'd seen my mother!"

"Do you know Mrs. Leslie?" asked Rosalie's mother, raising herself in bed.

"Yes, that I do," said the girl. "She's our minister's wife—such a kind lady—she *is* good to us! I'm in her Bible class. We go to the vicarage every Sunday afternoon. How do *you* know her?" she asked, turning to Rosalie's mother.

"I used to know her many years ago," said the sick woman. "But it's a long, long time since I saw her."

Rosalie crept up to her mother's side, and put her hand in hers. She knew that the mention of her sister Lucy would bring back all the sad memories of the past. But Rosalie's mother was very calm today, and did not seem at all ruffled or disturbed. She lay looking at Jessie with her eyes half closed. It seemed as if she were pleased even to look at someone who had seen her sister Lucy.

About six o'clock Toby was up, and he came to the caravan door, and asked how his mistress was, and if they were ready to start. He was very surprised when he saw Jessie sitting inside the caravan. Rosalie told him how the girl came there, and asked him in what direction she ought to walk to get to her own home. Toby was very clever in knowing the way to nearly every place in the country, and he said that for ten miles further their roads would be the same, and Jessie could ride with them in the caravan.

Jessie was very grateful to them for all their kindness. She sat beside Rosalie's mother all the morning, and did everything she could for her. But the effect of the doctor's medicine had passed, and the sick woman was very restless and wakeful. She was burning with fever, and tossed about from side to side on her bed. Every now and then her mind seemed to wander, and she talked of her mother and her sister Lucy, and of other things which Rosalie did not understand. Sometimes she would repeat over and over again the words of the hymn, or would ask Rosalie to read to her once more about the lost sheep and the good Shepherd.

When Rosalie had read the parable, her mother turned to Jessie.

"Do ask the Good Shepherd to find you now, Jessie. You'll be so glad afterwards!"

"But I've been so bad!" said Jessie in dismay. "My mother has often talked to me, and Mrs. Leslie has too; and yet now I've gone and done this. I daren't ever ask Him to find me *now!*"

"Why not, Jessie?" asked Rosalie's mother. "Why not *ask* Him?"

"Oh, He would have nothing to say to me," said the girl, hiding her face in her hands. "If I'd only gone to Him that Sunday!"

"What Sunday?" asked Rosalie.

"It was the Sunday before I left home. Mrs. Leslie talked to us about coming to Jesus. She asked if we had come to Him to have our sins forgiven; and she said, 'If you haven't come to Him already, come to Him today.' And then she begged those of us who hadn't come to Him before to go home when the class was over, and kneel down in our own rooms and ask Jesus to forgive us that very Sunday afternoon. I knew *I* had never come to Jesus, and I made up my mind that I would do as our teacher asked us. But, as soon as we were outside the vicarage, the girls began talking and laughing, and made fun of somebody's bonnet that they had seen in church that morning. And when I got home I thought no more of coming to Jesus, and I never went to Him—and oh! I wish that I had!"

The Dream

"Go now," said Rosalie's mother.

"It wouldn't be any good," said the girl sadly. "If I thought it would—if I only *thought* He would forgive me, I would do anything—I would walk *twice* the distance home!"

" 'He goeth after that which is lost until He find it," said the sick woman, repeating part of the Bible verse. "Are *you* lost, Jessie?"

"Yes," said the girl; "that's just what I am!"

"Then He is going after *you*," said Rosalie's mother again. "He loves you, Jessie."

Jessie walked to the door of the caravan, and sat looking out without speaking. The sunlight was streaming on the purple heather, which was spread like a carpet on both sides of the road. Quiet little roadside springs trickled through the moss and ran across the path. The travelers had left the pine forest behind, and there was not a single tree in sight. There was nothing but large grey rocks and occasional patches of bright yellow furze amongst the miles and miles of heath-covered moor.

At last they came to a large signpost, at a corner where four roads met. Toby said Jessie must leave them. Before she went there was a little whispered conversation between Rosalie and her mother, which ended in Jessie's taking away in her pocket no less than half the value of Mother Manikin's present.

"You'll need it before you get home, dear," said the sick woman, "and mind you go straight to your mother. Don't stop till you run right into her arms! And when you see Mrs. Leslie, just tell her you met with a woman in a caravan called Norah, who knew her many years ago."

"Yes," said Jessie, "I'll tell her!"

"And say that I sent my respects—my *love* to her. And

tell her I have not very long to live, but the Good Shepherd has sought me and found me, and I'm not afraid to die. Please don't forget to tell her that."

"No," said Jessie. "I'll be sure to remember."

The girl was very sorry to leave them. She kissed Rosalie and her mother, and as she went down the road she kept turning round to wave her handkerchief, till the caravan was out of sight.

"So those girls knew nothing about it, Rosalie darling," said her mother, when Jessie was gone.

"Nothing about what, Mother?" asked Rosalie.

"Don't you remember the girls that stood by our show when the procession went past? They wished they were Britannia."

"Oh yes!" said Rosalie. "I remember now. Yet all the time poor Jessie was so miserable she did not know what to do with herself. You *said* you thought she was unhappy."

"It's just the mistake *I* made, Rosalie darling, till I came behind the scenes and knew how different everything can look when one is there."

As evening drew on they left the moor, and turned into a very dark road with trees on both sides. Rosalie's mother was sleeping, for the first time since early morning, and Rosalie sat and looked out at the door of her yellow caravan. The wood was very thick, and the long shadows of the trees fell across the road. Every now and then they disturbed four or five rabbits, enjoying themselves by the side of the path. They would run headlong into their snug, little holes as soon as they heard the creaking of the caravan wheels. Then an owl startled Rosalie by hooting in a tree overhead, and several wood pigeons cooed mournfully their sad good nights.

The Dream

The road was full of turnings, and wound in and out amongst the wood. Toby whistled a tune as he went along, and Rosalie sat and listened to him, quite glad that he broke the silence. She was not sorry when they left the wood behind and came into the open country. And at last there glimmered in the distance the lights of a village, where Toby said they would spend the night. He pulled up the caravan by the wayside, and begged a bed for himself in a barn belonging to one of the small village farms.

The next day was Sunday. Such a calm, quiet day, the very air seemed full of rest. The country children were just going to the Sunday school as the caravan started on its way once more. Their mothers had carefully dressed the children in their best clothes, and were watching them down the village street.

The sick woman had had a restless and tiring night. Rosalie had watched beside her, and was now weary and sad. Her mother had tossed from side to side on her bed, and could find no position in which she was comfortable. Again and again Rosalie altered her mother's pillow, and tried to make her more comfortable. But, though she thanked her very gently, not many minutes had passed before she wanted to be moved again.

The Sunday stillness seemed to have a soothing effect, however; and, as they left the village, Rosalie's mother fell asleep. That sleep lasted for hours; and when she awoke she seemed refreshed and rested.

"Rosalie darling," she said. "I've had such a beautiful dream!"

"What was it?" asked Rosalie.

"I thought I was looking into Heaven, Rosalie dear, in between the bars of the golden gates. I saw people dressed in white walking up and down the streets of the city. And then somebody seemed to call them together, and they all went in one direction, and there was a beautiful sound of singing and joy, as if they had heard some good news. One of them passed close to the gate where I was standing, Rosalie, and he looked so happy and glad, as he was hurrying on to join the others. So I called him, and asked him what was going on."

"And what did he say?" asked Rosalie in hushed excitement, for the dream sounded so real to her.

"He said, 'It's the Good Shepherd who has called us. He wants us to rejoice with Him. He has just found one of the lost sheep, which He has been seeking so long. Did you not hear His voice just now, when He called us all together? Did you not hear Him saying: Rejoice with me, for I have found my sheep which was lost?'

"And then they all began to sing again and, somehow, I knew they were singing for *me*, and that *I* was the sheep that was found. And then I was so glad that I awoke with joy! And oh! Rosalie darling, I *know* my dream was true, for I've been asking Him to find me again and again, and I'm quite sure that He *wanted* to do it, long before I asked Him."

"Oh, Mother!" said Rosalie, putting her hand in her mother's, "I *am* so glad!"

Rosalie's mother did not talk any more then; but she lay very quietly, holding Rosalie's hand, and every now and then she smiled, as if the music of the heavenly song were still in her ears, and as if she still heard the Good Shepherd saying, "Rejoice with me, for I have found my sheep which was lost."

Then they passed through another village, where the bells were ringing for an afternoon service, and the sick woman listened to them, looking sad now.

"I shall never go to church again, Rosalie darling," she said.

"Oh, Mother!" said Rosalie. "Don't talk like that! When you get better we'll go together. We could easily slip into the back seats where nobody would see us."

"No, Rosalie," said her mother. "You may go, but *I* never shall."

"Why not?" asked a puzzled Rosalie.

"Rosalie," said her mother, raising herself in bed and putting her arm round her child, "don't you know that I'm going to leave you? Don't you know that in about a week's time you will have no mother?"

Rosalie hid her face in her mother's pillow. "Oh, Mother, dear Mother, don't say that! Please don't say that!" Then she began to cry.

"But it's true, little Rosalie," said her mother, "and I want you to know it. I don't want it to take you by surprise. And now stop crying, for I want to talk to you. I want to tell you some things whilst I can speak."

She stroked her girl's head very gently; and after a long, long time the crying ceased, and Rosalie listened quietly.

"Rosalie darling, you won't be sorry for your mother; will you, dear? The Good Shepherd has found me, and I'm going to see Him. I'm going to see Him, and thank Him, darling; you mustn't cry for me. And I want to tell you what to do. I've asked your father to let you leave the caravan, and live in some country village. But he won't give his consent, darling; he says he can't spare you. I've been asking the Good Shepherd to take care of you. I asked Him to put you in His arms and carry you along. And I believe He will, Rosalie dear; I don't think He'll let you go wrong. But you must ask Him yourself, my darling. You must never let a day pass without asking Him. Promise your mother, Rosalie—let me hear you say the words."

"Yes, Mother," said Rosalie quietly. "I promise."

"And if you can ever go to your Aunt Lucy you must give her that letter. You remember where it is; and tell her, dear, that I shall see her some day in that city I dreamt about. I should never have seen her if it had not been for the Shepherd's love. He took such pains to find me, and He wouldn't give up, and at last He put me on His shoulders and carried me home.

"I am very tired, Rosalie darling, but there is more that I wanted to say. I wanted to tell you that it will not do for you to ask your father about going to your Aunt Lucy, because he would never let you. He would only be writing to her for money if he knew where she lived. But if you go through that village again, you might just run up to the house and give her the letter. I believe you will get there some day. I can't talk any more now, darling, I am so tired."

Rosalie lifted up a very sorrowful face, and kissed her mother.

"You couldn't sing your little hymn, could you, darling?" said the sick woman.

Rosalie tried her very best to sing it. She struggled through the first verse, but in the second she broke down, and burst into a fresh flood of tears. Her mother tried to soothe her, but was too weak and weary to do more than stroke the girl's face with her thin hand, and whisper in her ear a few words of love.

Her mother was everything to Rosalie. She had never known a father's love or care—Augustus had never acted as a father to her. But her mother—her mother had been everything to her, from the day she was born until now.

Rosalie could not imagine what the world would be like without her mother. She could hardly fancy herself living when her mother was dead. She would have no one to speak to her, no one to care for her, no one to love her.

> Words of love Thy voice is speaking,
> "Come, come to Me."

What was it made her think of the hymn on the card just now? Was it not the Good Shepherd's voice, as He held the lonely lamb close to himself?

> Come, come to Me.

"Good Shepherd, I do come," said the weary Rosalie. "I come to you now!"

CHAPTER 12

Alone

T was Sunday evening when the caravan reached the town where the fair was to be held. The travelers passed numbers of people in their Sunday clothes, and saw many churches and chapels open for evening service as they drove through the town. The brightly painted caravan looked strangely out of keeping with everything around it on that evening.

Augustus met them as they reached the common which was already full of show people. The common was a large piece of ground on a cliff overlooking the sea.

Rosalie could hear the waves on the rocks below as she sat beside her mother that night. In the morning, as her mother was sleeping quietly, she stole out on the shore and wandered about amongst the rocks before the rest of the show people were awake.

A long ridge of rocks stretched out into the sea, and Rosalie walked along this, watching the restless waves as they dashed against it and broke into thick, white foam. In some parts the rocky way was covered with small limpets, whose shells crackled under Rosalie's feet. Then came some deep pools filled with green and red seaweed in which Rosalie discovered pink sea anemones and small, restless crabs. She examined one or two of these, but her heart was too sad to be interested by them long, so she wandered on until she reached the far end of the ridge of rocks. Here she sat for some time, gazing at the breakers, and watching the sunshine spreading over the silvery grey waters.

Her mother was awake when Rosalie got back to the caravan, but she seemed very weak and tired, and all that long day scarcely spoke.

In the afternoon the noise of the fair began: There was the rattling of the shooting galleries, the bells of the three large roundabouts and two noisy bands playing different tunes. This made a strange, discordant sound, an odd mixture of the "Mabel Waltz" and "Poor Mary Ann."

Then, as the crowds in the fair became denser, the shouts and noise increased on all sides. Augustus was far too busy preparing for the evening's entertainment to spend much time in his wife's caravan. He did not know, or he would not see, that a change was passing over her face. Thus, about half an hour before the theater opened, he called to Rosalie to dress herself for the play, and would listen to none of her pleading to stay with her mother.

So Rosalie dared not stay. Was not this the great fair her

father had been counting on all the year, and from which he hoped to reap the greatest profit? And had he not told her that if she broke down in her part in *this* town he would never forgive her as long as he lived?

No, there was no help for it; she must go. But not until the last moment—not until the very last moment would she leave her mother. She dressed very quickly, and sat down in her white dress beside her mother's bed.

"Rosalie," said her mother, "are you going—must you leave me?"

"Oh, Mother, it is so hard! It is so very, very hard!"

"Don't cry, my little lamb, don't cry! It's all right. Lift me up a little, Rosalie."

Rosalie altered her mother's pillows very gently, and then the sick woman whispered, "I'm close to the deep waters. I can hear the sound of them now. I've got to cross the river, Rosalie, but I'm not afraid. The Good Shepherd has laid me on His shoulder. I know He'll carry me through."

Rosalie could not speak; she could only kiss her mother's hand. And then came her father's call to her to make haste and come into the theater.

What happened in the theater that night Rosalie never exactly knew; it all seemed as a horrible dream to her. She said the words and acted her part; but she saw not the stage nor the spectators. After the first play was over, Rosalie darted swiftly out of the theater and into her mother's caravan, almost knocking over several people who were passing by, and who stared at her in astonishment.

Her mother smiled as she opened the door. How glad Rosalie was for that. But her mother did not seem to hear her speak, and her breathing was very painful. Rosalie bent over and gave her one long, long kiss, and then hurried back for the next performance just as her father began shouting for her.

When she next came into the caravan all was still. Her mother seemed to be sleeping more quietly, the painful breathing had ceased.

At last the theater shut for the night. Weary and aching in every limb, Rosalie fell asleep on the chair by her mother's side. When she awoke, she knew that the Good Shepherd had carried her mother safely over the river. As Rosalie wept in the dark caravan, He was even then welcoming her mother to the home above. He was even then saying, in tones of joy, yet more glad than before, "Rejoice with me; for I have found my sheep which was lost."

But Rosalie, poor motherless Rosalie. Had the Good Shepherd quite forgotten her? Was she left alone in her sorrow? No, the Good Shepherd drew near in that night of darkness. He cared for the lonely lamb. He whispered words of comfort and love to the weary, sorrowful Rosalie, and held her tightly in His arms of love.

It was the next morning. The sun had already risen and the show people were beginning to stir. The fishing boats were once more coming home, and the breakers were rolling on the shore. Augustus Joyce awoke with a strange feeling of uneasiness, for which he could not account. Nothing had gone wrong the night before. Rosalie had made no mistake in her part, and his profits had been larger than usual. And yet Augustus Joyce was not happy. He had had a dream the night before; perhaps that was the reason. He had dreamt of his wife; and it was not often that he dreamt of her now. He had dreamt of her, not as she was then, thin and very ill, but as she had been on their wedding day, when she had been his bride, and he had promised to take her "for better, for worse, for richer, for poorer, in sickness and in health, to love and to cherish her, till death do they part."

He hurried to the caravan, opened the door and entered. Immediately he understood what had happened. When Rosalie awoke, she found herself being lifted gently from the bed by her father, and carried into the other caravan. There he laid her on his own bed, and went out, shutting the door behind him.

The next few days seemed like one long night to Rosalie. Of the preparations for the funeral she knew nothing. She seemed like one in a dream. The fair went on all around her, and the noise made her more and more miserable. What she liked best was to hear the dull roaring of the sea, after the naphtha lights were out and all in the fair was still. In the early morning, Rosalie would stand on the beach and watch the waves.

Somehow—although Rosalie hardly knew how—the Good Shepherd comforted and soothed her. She knew that He loved her, and that He held her securely in His arms. Rosalie had called to the Good Shepherd, and He had found her. She belonged to Him.

CHAPTER 13

The Fair

"M ISS ROSIE, can I speak to you?" asked Toby, the day before the funeral.

"Yes. Come in, Toby," said Rosalie.

"I should like to see you, Miss Rosie," said Toby, mysteriously. "You won't be offended, will you? But I brought you this."

Then followed a great fumbling in Toby's pockets, and from the depths of one of them he produced a large, red handkerchief. When he had undone the various knots, he carefully took out a small packet, which he laid on Rosalie's knee.

"It's only a bit of black, Miss Rosie," he said. "I thought you could put it on tomorrow. And you mustn't mind my seeing to it. There was no one to do it but me."

Before Rosalie could thank him he was gone.

When she opened the packet she found in it a piece of broad black ribbon, and a black silk handkerchief—the best Toby could obtain. Rosalie fastened the ribbon on her hat, to be ready for the funeral service tomorrow.

All the company of the theater followed Augustus Joyce's wife to the grave, and more than one of them felt unusually moved as they looked at Rosalie walking by her father's side. She was calm and quiet, and never shed a tear until the service was over. Then her eyes fell upon Toby, who was walking near her with an air of heartfelt sorrow on his face. He had tied a piece of black ribbon round his own hat and a black handkerchief round his neck, out of respect for his late mistress and for his mistress's daughter.

Something in the curious way in which the black ribbon was fastened on, something in the thought of the kind Toby who had planned this token of sympathy, touched Rosalie, and brought tears to her eyes for the first time that day.

Then she burst into a flood of tears, and was able to weep out the intenseness of her sorrow. And after that came a calm into her heart; for, somehow, she felt as if the angels' song was not yet over, as if they were still singing for joy over her mother's soul, and as if Jesus, the Good Shepherd, was still saying, "Rejoice with me, for I have found my sheep which was lost."

Then they left the seaside town, and set off for a distant fair. Rosalie was very lonely in her caravan. Everywhere and in everything she felt a sense of loss. Her father occasionally came to see her; but his visits were anything but agreeable, and she always felt relieved when he went away again to his own caravan.

Rosalie often climbed beside Toby and watched him

driving, and spoke to him of the things they passed by the way. But the hours by night were the longest of all, when the caravan was drawn up on a lonely moor or in a thickly wooded valley. There was no sound to be heard but the hooting of the owls and the wind amongst the trees. Then Rosalie would kneel down and repeat her evening prayer again and again, and ask the Good Shepherd to keep her in His arms, now that she was so lonely.

At last they arrived at the fair for which they were bound. The acting went on as usual, and Rosalie had once more to take her place on the stage.

Everything seemed sad to her. Her white dress was soiled and tumbled now, and the wreath of roses looked crushed and faded, as Rosalie took it from the box. Her father came looking for her, and told her they were all waiting, and then the play commenced.

Rosalie's eyes wandered up and down the theater, and she thought of her mother, and of the different place where she was that very evening. Rosalie had been reading about it that afternoon before she dressed herself for the play. She thought of the streets of gold on which her mother was walking. She thought of the white robe in which her mother was dressed, so unlike this soiled dress. She thought of the new song her mother was singing, so different from the songs that were being sung in the theater.

She thought, too, of the words which her mother was saying to the Good Shepherd, perhaps even now, "Thou art worthy; for Thou wast slain, and hast redeemed me to God by thy blood." How she longed to be with her mother in the golden city, instead of in the hot, wearying theater!

So the weeks went on; fair after fair was visited; her father's new play was repeated again and again, till it seemed very old to Rosalie. The theater was set up and taken down, and all went on much as usual.

There was no change in Rosalie's life, except that she had found a new occupation and pleasure. And this was teaching Toby to read.

"Miss Rosie," he said one day, "I wish I could read that Bible of yours."

"Can't you read, Toby?"

"Not a word, missie; I only wish I could. Will you teach me?"

So Rosalie began to teach Toby to read. Every day she sat beside him, with her Bible in her hand, pointing out one word after another as they drove slowly along. And when Toby was tired of learning, Rosalie would read to him some story out of the Bible. The one they read more often than any other was the parable of the lost sheep. It had a special meaning to Rosalie, and Toby knew and understood this.

There was one thing for which Rosalie was very anxious, and that was to meet Mother Manikin again. At every fair they visited she looked with eager eyes for the Royal Show of Dwarfs. But they seemed to have taken a different circuit from that of the theater party. Fair after fair went by, and Rosalie began to give up hope. But at length one afternoon, the last afternoon of the fair, Toby came running to the caravan with an eager face.

"Miss Rosie," he said, "I've just found the Royal Show of Dwarfs. They're here, Miss Rosie. As soon as I caught sight of the picture over the door, I thought to myself, 'Miss Rosie will be glad.' So I went up to the door and spoke to the owner (they've got a new one, Miss Rosie), and he said they were leaving tonight. So I ran off at once to tell you—I knew you would like to see Mother Manikin again."

"Oh, Toby!" said Rosalie, "I am glad."

"You'll have to go at once, Miss Rosie. They're to start off tonight the moment the performance is over. They're due at another fair tomorrow."

"How was it that you didn't find them before, Toby?"

"I don't know how it was, Miss Rosie, except they're at the very far end of the fair, and I haven't happened to be down that way before. Now, Miss Rosie, if you like I'll take you."

"But I daren't leave the caravan, Toby. My father has the key. It wouldn't be safe, would it, to leave it unlocked with all these people around?"

"No," said Toby, as he looked down on the surging mass of people, "I don't suppose it would. You'd have all your things stolen, Miss Rosie."

"What shall I do?"

"Well, if you wouldn't mind going by yourself, Miss Rosie, I'll keep guard here."

"Where is it, Toby?" Rosalie asked.

"Right at the other end of the field, Miss Rosie. Do you hear that clanging noise?"

"Yes," said Rosalie. "Very well. It sounds as if all the tin trays in the town were being thrown one upon another!"

"That's the giant's cave, Miss Rosie, where that noise is, and the dwarf show is close by. Keep that noise in your ears, and you will be sure to find it."

So Rosalie left Toby in the caravan, and went down into the pushing crowd. It was in the middle of the afternoon, and the fair was full of people. They were going in different directions, and it was hard work for Rosalie to get through them.

A long row of brightly painted shows was on the one side of her, and at the door of each stood a man calling to the crowd, and boasting of the special attractions of his show. First there were the waxworks, with a row of figures outside.

"Ladies and gentlemen, here is the most select show in the fair! Here is amusement and instruction combined! Here is nothing to offend the moral and artistic taste! You may see here Abraham offering up Aaron, and Henry IV in prison, Cain and Abel in the garden of Eden, and William the Conqueror driving out the ancient Britons!"

Then, as Rosalie pressed on through the crowd, she was jostled in front of the show of the giant boy and girl. Here there was a great crowd of people, gazing at the huge picture of an enormously fat Highlander, which was hung over the door. In front of this show was a man beating a drum with his right hand and turning a barrel organ with his left, and another man blowing loudly through a trumpet. In spite of all this noise, a third man was standing on a raised platform, and calling to the crowds beneath.

"I say, I say! Now exhibiting, the great Scotch brother and sister, the greatest ever exhibited! All for twopence; all for twopence! children half price! You're *just* in time, you're in capital time; I'm so glad to see you in such good time. Come on now, take your seats, take your seats!"

Rosalie struggled on, but another enormous crowd stopped her way. This time it was in front of the show of Marionettes, or dancing dolls. On the platform outside the show was a man shaking a puppet which was dressed in a suit of armor.

"These are not *living* actors, ladies and gentlemen," cried the man outside. "Yet if you come inside you will see wonderfully artistic feats! None of the figures are alive, which makes the performance so much more interesting and pleasing. Now's your chance, ladies and gentlemen! Now's your chance! There's plenty of room! It isn't often I can tell you so; it is the rarest occurrence. But now there *is* room! Now's your chance!"

Past all these shows Rosalie pushed, longing to get on, yet unable to hurry. Then she came to a corner of the fair where a man with a tray was crying his wares.

"Here's a watch," said the man, holding it up. "Cost me two pounds ten shillings! I couldn't let you have it for a penny less! I'll give anyone five pounds that will get me a watch like this for two pounds ten in any shop in the town. Come now, anyone say two pounds ten?" giving a great slap on his knee. "Two pounds ten shillings! Two pounds ten shillings! Well, I'll tell you what: I'll take off the two pounds, I'll say ten shillings! Come, ten shillings! Ten shillings! Ten shillings! Well, I'll be generous, I'll say five shillings; I'll take off a crown. Come now, five shillings!" This was said with another tremendous slap on his knee. Then, without stopping a moment, he went from five shillings to four-and-sixpence, four shillings, three-and-sixpence.

"Well, I don't mind telling my dearest relation and friend, that I'll let you have it for two-and-six. Come now, two shillings and sixpence; two shillings; one-and-six; one shilling; sixpence. Come now, sixpence! Only sixpence!"

At this a boy held out his hand, and became for sixpence the possessor of the watch, which the man had declared only two minutes before he would not part with for less than two pounds ten shillings!

Rosalie looked puzzled, but pressed on and turned the corner. Here there was another row of shows. A fat boy, some of whose huge clothes were being paraded outside as an example of what was to be seen within; the lady without arms, whose wonderful feats of knitting, sewing, writing, and tea making were being told to the crowd; the entertaining theater, outside which was a stuffed performing cat playing on a drum, and two tiny children, both about three years old, dressed in the most extraordinary costumes and dancing with tambourines in their hands; the picture gallery, in which the crowds were told they could see Adam and Eve, Queen Elizabeth, and other distinguished persons—all these were on Rosalie's right hand, and on her left was a long succession of stalls, on which were sold gingerbread, brandysnap, nuts, biscuits, coconuts, boiled peas, hot potatoes, and sweets of all kinds. Here was a man selling cheap walking sticks, and there was another offering the boys a moustache and a pair of spectacles for a penny each and assuring them that if they would only lay down the small sum of twopence they might become the greatest swells in the town.

Rosalie was relieved to get past them all, and to hear the clanging sound from the giant's cave growing nearer and nearer. At last, to her joy, she arrived before the Royal Show of Dwarfs. "Now," she thought, "I shall see Mother Manikin."

The performance was just about to begin, and the owner was standing at the door inviting people to enter.

"Now, miss," he said, turning to Rosalie, "now's your time; only a penny, and none of them more than three feet high! Showing now! Showing now!"

Rosalie paid the money, and pressed eagerly into the show. The little people had just appeared, and were bowing and paying compliments to the company. But Mother Manikin was not there. Rosalie's eyes wandered up and down the show, and peered behind the curtain at the end, but Mother Manikin was nowhere to be seen. Rosalie could not enjoy the performance, so anxious was she to know if her little friend was within. At last the entertainment was over, and the giant and dwarfs shook hands with the company before ushering them out.

Rosalie was the last to leave, and when the tall, thin giant came up to her she said, "Please, *may* I see Mother Manikin?"

"Who are you, my child?" asked the giant, majestically.

"I'm Rosalie—Rosalie Joyce. Don't you remember that Mother Manikin sat up with my mother when she was ill?"

"Oh dear me! Yes, I remember it; of course I do," said the giant.

"Of course, of course," echoed the three dwarfs, who had gathered round.

"Then please will you take me to Mother Manikin?"

"With the greatest of pleasure, if she were here," said the giant with a bow. "But the unfortunate part of the business is that she is *not* here!"

"No, she's not here," said the dwarfs.

"Oh dear! oh dear!" said Rosalie, with a little cry of disappointment.

"Very sorry, indeed, my dear," said the giant. "I suppose *I* shan't do instead?"

"No," said Rosalie, "it was Mother Manikin I wanted; she knew all about my mother."

"Very sorry indeed, my dear," repeated the giant.

"Very sorry, very sorry!" echoed the dwarfs.

"Where *is* Mother Manikin?" asked Rosalie.

"Why, the fact is, my dear, she has retired from the show. Made her fortune, you see. At least, having saved a nice sum of money, she determined to leave the show. Somehow, she grew tired of entertaining company, and told us 'old age must have its liberties.' "

"Then where is she?" asked Rosalie with a smile, even though she felt anxious.

"She has taken rooms in a town in the south of the county—very comfortable, my dear. You must call and see her some day."

"Oh dear!" said Rosalie; "I'm so very, very sorry she is not here!"

"Poor girl," said the giant kindly.

"Poor girl! poor girl!" said the dwarfs.

Rosalie turned to go, but the giant waved her back. "A cup of tea?"

"Oh no," said Rosalie. "I must go, thank you. Toby is keeping guard for me. I mustn't stay a minute."

"Won't you?" said the giant, reproachfully. "Then goodbye, my dear. I wish I could escort you home, but we mustn't make ourselves too cheap, you know. Goodbye, goodbye!"

"Goodbye, my dear. Goodbye!" called out the dwarfs.

Rosalie turned homewards, and struggled through the surging mass of people. The owner of the show had pointed out a shortcut to the theater caravan. She was glad to get out of the clanging sound of the giant's cave, from the platform where a man was assuring the crowd that if only they would come to this show they would be sure to come again that very evening, and would bring *all* their friends with them!

Then Rosalie went through a long covered bazaar, in which a multitude of toys, wax dolls, wooden dolls, china dolls, composition dolls, rag dolls, and dolls of all descriptions were displayed together with wooden horses, donkeys, elephants, and every kind of toy. After this she came upon a more open space, where a happy family was being displayed to an admiring throng. It consisted of a large cage fastened to a cart, which was drawn by a donkey. Inside the cage were various animals, living on the most friendly terms with each other—a little dog in a smart coat, playing with several small, white rats; a monkey hugging a white kitten; a white cat which had been dyed a brilliant yellow, playing gently with a number of mice and dormice; and a duck, a hen, and a guinea pig, which were sitting together in one corner of the cage. Over this show a board announced that this happy family was supported entirely by voluntary contributions; and a woman was going about amongst the crowd shaking a tin plate at them, and crying out against their stinginess if they refused to contribute.

Rosalie passed the happy family with difficulty, and made her way through another part of the fair. On one side of her were shooting galleries, which made a deafening noise, and on the other were all manner of stalls and sideshows.

There were the weighing machines, armchairs covered with red velvet (in which you were invited to sit and be weighed). There was the sponge dealer—a Turk in a turban, who confided to the crowd in broken English not only the price of his sponges, but also many interesting details of his personal history. There was also the usual gathering of professional beggars, some without arms and legs, others deaf, or dumb, or blind, or all three. There were cripples and simple folk, who went from fair to fair and town to town, begging.

Rosalie went quickly past them all, and came upon the roundabouts and rides, four or five of which were at work, and were whirling in different directions, and made her feel so dizzy that she hardly knew where she was going.

How glad she was to see her own bright yellow caravan

again—to get safely out of the noisy crowd! Toby was looking anxiously for her from the window.

"Miss Rosie," he said. "I thought you were never coming. I got quite frightened about you. You're such a little mite of a thing to go fighting your own way in that great, big crowd!"

"Oh, Toby," said Rosalie. "I haven't seen Mother Manikin!" And she told him what she had heard from the giant.

"I am sorry," said Toby. "Then you have had all your walk for nothing?"

"Yes," said Rosalie. "I wonder if I shall *ever* see my friend again!"

CHAPTER 14

Betsey Ann

HERE was still some time before Rosalie would need to dress for the play. She sat still after Toby had left, thinking over all she had seen in the fair.

Suddenly she heard a sound close to her, a very different sound from the shouting of the stallholders or the noisy boasting of the showmen. It was the sound of singing. She went to the door of the caravan and looked out.

The theater was set up at the edge of the fair. Close to the street, and very near the caravan—so near that Rosalie could hear all they said—stood a group of men. One of them had just given out a hymn, and they were all singing it. Rosalie could hear every word distinctly. There was a chorus at the end of each verse, and before the hymn was finished she knew it by heart.

Betsey Ann

Whosoever will, whosoever will;
Sound the proclamation over vale and hill;
'Tis a loving Father calls His children home;
  Whosoever will may come!

By the time they finished the first verse, a great crowd had collected round the men, attracted by the contrast between the hymn and the din and tumult in every other part of the fair.

Then one of the men began to speak. "Friends," he said. "Friends, I have an invitation for you tonight. Will you listen to my invitation? You are being invited in all directions tonight. Each man invites you to his own show, and tells you it is the best one in the fair. Each time you pass him he calls out to you, 'Come! come! Come now! Now's your time!'

"My friends, I too have an invitation for you tonight. I too would say to you, 'Come! come! Come now! Now's your time!' Jesus Christ, my friends, has sent me with this invitation to you. He wants you to *come*. He says, *'Come unto me, all ye that labor and are heavy laden.'* He wants you to come *now*. He says, 'Come *now*, let us reason together; though your sins be as scarlet, they shall be as white as snow.'

"My friends, this is the invitation; but it is a very different one from the one that man is giving at that show over there. What does he say to those people who are listening to him just now? Does he say, 'Here's my show; the door is open, anyone who likes may walk in; there's nothing to pay'? Does he say that? No, my friends; he always follows up his 'Come, come now! now's your time!' with some such words as these, 'Only twopence; only twopence; only twopence to pay! Come now!' And, if you do not produce your twopence, will he let you in? If you are so poor that you have not twopence in the world, will he say to you, 'Come, come now! now's your time'? No, my friends, that he will *not* do!

"Now the Lord Jesus Christ invites you quite differently. He cries out! 'Ho! everyone that thirsteth, come. Come without money! Come without price! Whosoever will may come!' Yes, my friends, the words 'Whosoever will' are written over the door which the Lord Jesus Christ wants you to enter. This is one way in which His invitation is quite different from the one which that man is giving from the door of the show.

"We will sing another verse of the hymn, and then I will tell you the other great difference between the two invitations."

So again they sang, and ended with the chorus:

> Whosoever will, whosoever will;
> Sound the proclamation over vale and hill;
> 'Tis a loving Father calls His children home;
> Whosoever will may come.

"My friends," said the speaker, as the crowd became silent, "the world's grandest display is a very disappointing thing. And this is the second way in which the Lord Jesus Christ's invitation is so different from that of the man at that show door. When the Lord Jesus Christ says 'Come,' He always has something good to give, something that is solid, something that will last, something that will not disappoint you. He has pardon to give you; He has peace to give you; He has Heaven to give you. All these are good gifts; all these will last; not one of them will disappoint you.

"Will *you* come to Him? He calls to you 'Come! come now!' Now's your time! There's room now; there is plenty of room now! Even now, there is room. Will you not come to Him tonight?

"Whosoever cometh need not delay;
Now the door is open: enter while you may;
Jesus is the true, the only living way;
  Whosoever will may come.

"Whosoever will, whosoever will;
Sound the proclamation over vale and hill;
'Tis a loving Father calls His children home;
  Whosoever will may come!"

"Rosalie," said her father's voice suddenly. "Be quick and get ready." Rosalie had to close the caravan door and dress for the play. But the hymn and the sermon were treasured up in her heart, and were never forgotten.

That was the last fair which Augustus Joyce visited that year. The cold weather was coming on. Already there had been one or two severe frosts, and the snow had come beating down the caravan chimney, almost extinguishing the fire in the iron stove.

Augustus thought it was high time he sought winter quarters. Having got a booking for himself in a town theater in the south for the winter months, he determined to go at once, and dismiss his company until the spring.

On the road to the large town they passed many other caravans, all bound on the same errand, coming like swallows to a warmer climate.

Rosalie's father went first to a stableyard, where the caravans were stowed away for the winter. Here he left Rosalie for some time, whilst he went to look for lodgings in the town. Then he and the men removed from the caravans the things which they would need, and carried them to their new quarters. When all was arranged, Augustus told Rosalie to follow him, and led the way through the town.

Rosalie wondered to what kind of place she was going. They went down several streets, wound in and out of different squares and courts, and Rosalie had to run every now and then to keep up with her father's long strides. At last they came to a winding street full of tall, gloomy houses. Her father stopped and knocked at a door. Some ragged children, without shoes or stockings, were sitting on the steps, and moved off as Rosalie and her father came up.

The door was opened by a girl about fifteen years old with a tired, careworn face. She was dressed in an untidy, torn frock which had lost all its hooks, and was fastened with large, white pins.

"Where's your mistress?" said Augustus Joyce.

The girl led the way to the back of the house, and opened the door of a dismal parlor. Rosalie gazed round her at the dirty paper on the walls, and the greasy chair covers and the ragged carpet.

Then the door opened, and the mistress of the house entered. She was an actress, Rosalie felt sure of that the first moment she saw her. She was dressed in a faded silk dress, which swept up the dust of the floor as she walked, and she greeted her new lodgers with an overpowering bow.

She took Rosalie upstairs, past several landings, where doors opened and people peered out to catch a glimpse of the new lodger, up to a little attic room in the roof, which was to be Rosalie's sleeping place. It was full of boxes, which the lady of the house had stowed there to be out of the way.

In one corner the boxes were pushed to one side, and a mattress was put there for Rosalie to sleep on, and a china basin was set on one of the boxes for her to wash in.

Rosalie's own box was already there. Her father had brought it up for her before she arrived, and she was pleased to find that it was still tied tightly with cord. There were treasures in that box which no one in that house must see!

The lady of the house told Rosalie that in a few minutes her supper would be ready, and that she must make haste and come downstairs. So Rosalie took off her hat and coat, and went down the many stairs to a room in the front of the house, where tea was provided for the lodgers.

Rosalie was most thankful when the meal was over. The loud voices and noisy laughter of the company grated on her ears, and she longed to make her escape. As soon as she could, she slipped from her father's side, and crept upstairs to her attic room. Here at least she could be alone and quiet. It was very cold, so she unfastened the box and took out her mother's shawl, which she wrapped tightly round her.

Then Rosalie opened out her treasures, and stowed them away as best she could. She opened the locket and looked at the young, girlish face inside. How she wished she was with her Aunt Lucy! Would she ever be able to keep that locket safely? That was her next thought. There was no key to the attic door, nor was there a key to her box. How could she be sure, when she was out at the theater, that the people of the house would not look through the contents of her box?

It was clear that the locket must be hidden somewhere safe. Rosalie would never forgive herself if, after her mother had kept it safely all those years, she should be the one to lose it. She sat for some time thinking how she should hide it, and then realized that the only safe way would be to wear it night and day round her neck underneath her dress, and never on any account to let anyone catch sight of it.

Rosalie tied the locket carefully in a small parcel, in which she placed the precious letter which her mother had written to her Aunt Lucy. Then, tying it round her neck, she hid the packet inside her dress.

After this Rosalie felt more easy, and unpacked her clothes, hanging them on some nails on the attic door. Then she took from her pocket her small, black Bible and crept up to the window to read a few verses before it was too dark. The light was fading fast and the lamplighter was going down the street lighting the lamps. There was no time to lose, for there was no candle in her room.

Rosalie began to read. "Casting all your care upon Him, for He careth for you."

She repeated these words over and over again to herself, so she would be able to remember them when the attic was dark. And they seemed just the words Rosalie needed. They were the Good Shepherd's words of comfort. He was whispering now to *her!*

But, as the shadows grew deeper and the room became darker, Rosalie suddenly felt very lonely and miserable. Once she thought she would go downstairs to look for her father; but whenever she opened the door there seemed to be so many people below that she did not like to leave the attic. She could not read now, and it was very cold indeed at the top of the house. Rosalie shivered from head to foot, and wondered if the long hours would ever pass away. At last she determined to get into bed, for she thought she should be warmer there, and hoped she might get to sleep. But it was still early, and sleep seemed far away.

Then Rosalie thought of her text, " 'Casting all your care upon Him, for He careth for you.' 'All *your* care'—that means *my* care," thought the weary girl. "*My* own care. '*All* your care—*all*—all the care about losing my mother, and about having to stay in this noisy house, and about having to go and act in that theater, and about having to take care of my locket and my letter.

" 'Casting all your care upon *Him,*' that means Jesus, my own Good Shepherd, who loves me so. I wonder what casting it on Him means," thought Rosalie. "How can I cast it on Him? If my mother was here I would tell her all about it, and ask her to help me. Perhaps that's what I've got to do to the Good Shepherd. I'll try."

So Rosalie knelt up in bed and said, "Good Shepherd, please, I want to speak to you. Please, I'm very lonely, and I'm so afraid someone will get my locket. Please keep it safe. And I'm so frightened in the dark in this nasty house. Please take care of me. I want to love you, dear Good Shepherd, and I want to meet my mother in Heaven. Please let me; and wash my sins away in the blood of Jesus. Amen."

Then Rosalie lay down again, and felt much happier. The pain at her heart seemed to be gone.

"He careth for you." How comforting those words of the text were! She did not have her mother to care for her, but the Good Shepherd cared for her. He loved her. He would not let her be alone. He would stay with her day and night.

Rosalie was thinking of this and repeating her text again, when she felt something moving on the bed, and something very cold touched her hand. She started back at first, but, in a moment, she found it was nothing but the nose of a little soft, furry kitten that had crept in through the door. Rosalie had left her door open a little, to get a ray of light from the gas lamp on the lower landing. The kitten seemed very cold, and Rosalie felt that it was as lonely as she was. She put it in a snug place in her arms and stroked it very gently, till the tiny creature purred softly with delight.

Rosalie had been lying still for some time, when she heard a step on the stairs, and her father's voice called, "Rosalie, where are you?"

"I'm in bed," said Rosalie.

"Oh! all right," said her father. "I couldn't find you. Good night."

Then he went downstairs, and Rosalie lay stroking the kitten, and wondering if she should ever get to sleep. It seemed as if it would never be bedtime—at least the bedtime for the people downstairs. The talking and laughing still went on, and Rosalie thought it would never cease.

But at last the weary hours went by, and the people seemed to be going to bed. Then the light on the landing was put out, and all was still. The kitten was fast asleep; and Rosalie at length followed its example, and dropped into a peaceful slumber.

She had been asleep a long, long time, at least so it seemed to her, when she woke up suddenly, and, opening her eyes, she saw a girl standing by her bedside with a candle in her hand. It was the maid who had opened the door for her and her father.

"What is it?" asked Rosalie, sitting up in bed. "Is it time to get up?"

"No," said the girl; "I'm only just coming to bed."

"Why, isn't it very late?" asked Rosalie.

"Late! I should think it *is* late," said the maid. "It's always late when *I* come to bed. I have to wash the pots after all the others have gone upstairs. Ay! but my back does ache tonight! Bless you! I've been upstairs and downstairs all day long."

"Who are you?" asked Rosalie.

"Is it time to get up?"

"I'm the kitchen maid here," said the girl. "I sleep in the other attic room next to you. Why did you go to bed so early?"

"I wanted to be by myself," explained Rosalie. "There was such a noise downstairs."

"La! do you call *that* a noise?" said the girl. "It's nothing to what there is sometimes. I thought they were pretty peaceful tonight!"

"Do you like being here?" asked Rosalie.

"Like it!" said the girl. "Bless you! Did you say *like* it? I hate it. I wish I could die. It's nothing but work, work, scold, scold, from morning till night!"

"Poor thing!" said Rosalie. "What is your name?"

"Betsey Ann," said the girl, with a laugh. "They gave me it in the workhouse. I was born there, and my mother died when I was born. I wish *I* was dead!"

"Will you go to Heaven when you die?" asked Rosalie.

"La! bless you, I don't know," said the girl. "I suppose so."

"Has the Good Shepherd *found* you yet?" asked Rosalie, "because if He hasn't, you won't go to Heaven, you know." To Rosalie this was such a natural question to ask, for she knew that the Good Shepherd had found *her*.

The girl stared at Rosalie with a bewildered air of amazement and surprise.

"Don't you *know* about the Good Shepherd?" persisted Rosalie.

"Bless you, I don't know anything," said the girl. "Nothing but my ABCs."

"I can read to you about it, or are you too tired?"

"No, not if it's not very long."

"Oh! it's short enough. I've got my Bible safe here under my pillow."

So Rosalie read the parable of the lost sheep; and the girl put her candle on one of the boxes and listened.

"It's very nice," she said when Rosalie had finished, "but I don't know what it means."

"Jesus is the Good Shepherd," said Rosalie. "You know who *He* is, don't you, Betsey Ann?"

"Yes, He's God, isn't He?"

"Yes, and He loves *you,*" said Rosalie openly.

"*Loves* me?" said Betsey Ann. "I don't believe He does. There's nobody loves *me*, and nobody never did!"

"Jesus does," said Rosalie.

"Well I never!" said the girl. "Where is He? What's He like?"

"He's up in Heaven," said Rosalie, "and yet He's in this room now, and He does loves you, Betsey Ann; I *know* He does."

"How do you know? Did He tell you?"

"Yes, He says in this book that He loved you, and died that you might go to Heaven. You couldn't have gone to heaven if He hadn't died."

"Bless you! I wish I knew as much as you do," said the girl.

"Will you come up here sometimes, and I'll read to you?" said Rosalie.

"La! catch missis letting me! She won't let me wink scarcely! I never get a minute to myself, week in and week out."

"I don't know what I can do, then," said Rosalie. "Could you come on Sunday?"

"Bless you, Sunday! Busiest day in the week here! Lodgers are all in, and want hot dinners!"

"Then I can't see a way at all," said Rosalie.

"I'll tell you what," said the girl. "I'll get up ten minutes earlier, and go to bed ten minutes later, if you'll read to me out of that book, and tell me about somebody loving *me*. Ten minutes in the morning and ten minutes at night. That will be twenty minutes a day!"

"I'd like that," said Rosalie.

"But I get up awful early," said Betsey Ann, "afore ever there's a glimmer of light. Would you mind being waked up before five o'clock?"

"Oh, not a bit," said Rosalie, "if only you'll come."

"I'll come sure enough," said the girl. "I like you!"

She took up her candle and was preparing to depart when she caught sight of the kitten's tail peeping out from Rosalie's pillow.

"La! bless you, there's that kitten!"

"Yes," said Rosalie, "we're keeping each other company."

"I should think it's glad to have a bit of quiet," said Betsey Ann. "It gets nothing but kicks all day long, and it's got no mother—she was found dead in the coal cellar last week. It's been pining for her ever since."

"Poor little thing!" said Rosalie; and she held it close. Being motherless was a link of sympathy between her and the kitten. She would pet and comfort that kitten as much as ever she could.

Then Betsey Ann wished Rosalie goodnight, took her candle, and went to her own attic room, dragging her feet wearily.

And Rosalie went back to sleep.

CHAPTER 15

The Lodging House

RUE to her promise, Betsey Ann appeared in the attic the next morning at ten minutes to five. She only had four hours' sleep, and she rubbed her eyes vigorously to make herself wide awake, before she attempted to wake Rosalie. Then she put her candle on the box and looked at the sleeping girl. Rosalie was lying with one arm under her cheek, and the other round the kitten. It seemed a shame to wake her; but the precious ten minutes were going fast, and it was Betsey Ann's only chance of hearing more of what had so roused her curiosity the night before.

To be loved was quite a new idea to the workhouse child. She had been fed, and clothed, and provided for, to a certain extent; but no one in the whole world had ever done anything for Betsey Ann through love. Caring love was an

132

experience which had never been hers. And yet there had
been a strange fascination to her in those words Rosalie had
spoken so simply the night before: "He loves you so much."
So, here she was, to discover some more about it. She gave
Rosalie's hand, the hand which was holding the kitten, a
very gentle tap.

"I say," she said, "I say, the ten minutes are going!"

The sleepy Rosalie turned over, and said, dreamily, "I'll
come in a minute, father; have you begun?"

"No; it's me," said the girl. "It's me. It's Betsey Ann.
Don't you remember you said you would read to me? Bless
me, I wish I hadn't waked you, you look so tired!"

"Oh yes, I remember," said Rosalie, sitting up. "I'm
awake now. How many minutes are there left?"

"Oh, seven or eight at most," said Betsey Ann, with a nod.

"Then we mustn't lose a moment," said Rosalie, pulling
her Bible from under her pillow.

"La! I wish I was a good scholar like you," said Betsey
Ann, as Rosalie quickly turned over the pages, and found a
verse she had already decided to read to her new friend, the
kitchen maid.

"For ye know the grace of our Lord Jesus Christ, that,
though He was rich, yet for your sakes He became poor, that
ye through His poverty might be rich."

"Isn't that a beautiful verse?" said Rosalie. "I used to read
it to my mother."

"Tell me about it," said Betsey Ann. "Put it plain for me."

" 'Ye know,' " said Rosalie, "that's how it begins. *You*
don't know, Betsey Ann, but you will soon, won't you?"

"La! yes," said the girl, "I hope I shall." But she sounded
rather unsure.

" 'Ye know the grace.' I'm not quite sure what grace

means. I was thinking about it the other day; and now that my mother's dead I've no one to ask about things. But I think it must mean love. It seems as if it ought to mean love in this verse; and He *does* love us, you know, Betsey Ann, so we can't be far wrong if we say it means love—love we don't deserve."

" 'Ye know the love of our Lord Jesus Christ'—that's the One we talked about last night, the One who loves you, Betsey Ann. 'That though He was rich,' that means He lived in Heaven, and had ever so many angels to wait on Him, and everything He wanted, all bright and shining, 'Yet, for your sakes,' that means *your* sake, Betsey Ann, just as much as if it had said, 'You know the love of the Lord Jesus Christ, that, though He was rich, yet for Betsey Ann's sake He became poor.' "

"Well, I never!" said Betsey Ann.

"Poor," repeated Rosalie. "So poor, my mother said, He hadn't a house, and had to tramp about from one place to another, and had to work in a carpenter's shop, and used to be hungry just like we are."

"Well, I never!" said Betsey Ann. "Whatever did He do that for?"

"That's the end of the verse," said Rosalie. " 'That ye through His poverty might be rich.' That is, He came to be poor and die, that *you* might be rich and go to live up where He came from—up in the city of gold, and live with Him always there."

Betsey Ann opened her eyes wider and wider in astonishment. "Well, now! I never heard the like! Why didn't nobody never tell me nothing about it afore?"

"I don't know," said Rosalie. "Is the time up?"

"Very near," said Betsey Ann, with a sigh. "There's lots to

do afore missis is up. There's all the rooms to sweep out, and all the fires to light, and all the breakfasts to set, and all the boots to clean."

"Can you wait one minute more?" asked Rosalie anxiously.

"Yes," said Betsey Ann. "Bless you, I can wait two or three. I'll take my shoes off so I can run quickly downstairs. That will save some time."

"I just wanted you to speak to the Lord Jesus before you go," said Rosalie.

"*Me* speak to Him! Why, bless you, I don't know how!"

"Kneel down," said Rosalie. "He's in the room, Betsey Ann, though you can't see Him, and He'll hear every word we say. *I'll* pray if you like."

Betsey Ann just nodded, so Rosalie smiled reassuringly at her, then said quietly, "Lord Jesus, thank you very much for leaving the gold city for us. Thank you for coming to be poor, and for loving us, and for dying for us. Please help Betsey Ann love you. Amen."

"I shall think about it all day; I declare I shall!" said Betsey Ann, as she took off her old shoes and prepared to run downstairs. "My word, I wonder nobody never told me afore!"

When Rosalie went down to breakfast that morning, she found her father and the lady of the house in conversation over the fireplace in the best parlor. They stopped talking when she came into the room, and her father welcomed her with a theatrical bow.

"Good morning, madam," he said. "I'm glad to find that you have benefited by your nocturnal slumbers."

Rosalie walked up to the fire with the kitten in her arms, and the lady of the house gave her a condescending kiss, and then took no further notice of her.

It was a strange life for Rosalie in the lodging house, with no one to speak kindly to her all day long but poor Betsey Ann.

Clatter, clatter, clatter, went Betsey Ann's old shoes, upstairs and downstairs, backwards and forwards, hither and thither. Sweeping and dusting, and cleaning, and washing up dishes from morning till night, went poor Betsey Ann. Whenever she stopped for a minute, her mistress's voice was heard screaming from the dingy parlor, "Betsey Ann, you lazy girl! What are you up to now?"

That afternoon, as Rosalie was sitting reading in her attic room, she heard the clattery shoes coming upstairs, and presently Betsey Ann entered the room.

"There's a boy wants to speak to you below," she said. "Can you come down?"

Rosalie hastened downstairs, and found Toby standing in the passage, his hat in his hand.

"Miss Rosie, beg pardon," he said, "but I've come to say goodbye."

"Oh, Toby! Are you going away?"

"Yes," said Toby. "Master doesn't want us any more this winter. He's got no work for us, so he has sent us off. I'm right sorry to go, I'm sure I am."

"Where are you going, Toby?"

"I can't tell, Miss Rosie," he said, with a shrug of his shoulders. "Where I can get work, I suppose."

"Oh, I *am* sorry you must go," said Rosalie.

"I shall forget all my learning," said Toby, mournfully. "But I tell you what, Miss Rosie, I shall be back here in spring. Master will take me on again, if I turn up in good time, and then you'll teach me a bit more reading, won't you? *And* you'll tell me more from that Bible of yours!"

"Yes," said Rosalie, "to be sure, I will. But, Toby, you won't forget *everything*, will you?"

"No, Miss Rosie," said Toby, "that I won't! It's always coming in my mind. I can't curse and swear now as I used to do. Somehow the bad words seem as if they would choke me. The last time I swore, I was in a row with one of our men, and out came some words, quite quick, before I thought of them. But the next minute, Miss Rosie, it all came back to me—all about the Good Shepherd, and how you said He was looking for me. Well, I ran out of the caravan, and I tried to forget it; but somehow it seemed as if the Good Shepherd was looking at me quite sorrowful like; and I couldn't be happy, Miss Rosie, not until I'd asked Him to forgive me."

"I'm glad," said Rosalie. "If you love the Good Shepherd, and don't like to hurt Him anymore, I think He must have already found you, Toby."

"Well, I don't know, Miss Rosie. I hope so, I'm sure. But I must be off. Only I couldn't go without bidding you goodbye. You've been so good to me, Miss Rosie, and taught me all I know."

After this, Rosalie's life went on much the same from day to day. Every morning she was awakened by Betsey Ann, and she read and explained a fresh verse from her Bible. Rosalie chose the verses the night before, and put a mark in the place so that she could begin to read the moment she awoke. And so, not one of the ten minutes was wasted.

Betsey Ann always listened with open mouth and eyes. And she did not listen in vain. There was a ray of sunshine, which lighted up her unhappy life, and made even poor Betsey Ann have something worth living for.

"He loves me," was the one idea which was firmly fixed in

her mind. "He loves me so much that He died for me." And that thought was enough to make even the dismal lodging house and the hard life seem less dark and dreary than before.

Very slowly, a change came over the girl, which Rosalie could not help noticing. She was gentler than she used to be, more quiet and patient. And she was happier, too. She seemed to be trying to learn about the Good Shepherd, who had done so much for her.

The short morning times together with Betsey Ann were the happiest part of Rosalie's days. She did not like the people she met in the large lodging house. They were very noisy, so she kept out of their way as much as possible. Many of them were actors and actresses, who stayed in bed till nearly dinnertime. So the morning was the quietest time. Even the lady of the house herself was often not up.

Rosalie would sit with the kitten on her knee in front of the fire in the parlor, thinking of her mother and of her Aunt Lucy, and making sure, every now and then, that her precious locket and letter were safe round her neck.

The kitten had a happy life. Rosalie always saved something from her own meals for it. Many a saucerful of bread and milk, many a dinner of gravy and pieces of meat did the kitten enjoy. And every night when Rosalie went to bed it was wrapped up in a warm shawl, and went to sleep in her arms. Wherever Rosalie was to be found, the kitten was to be found also. It followed her upstairs and downstairs. It crept to her feet when she sat at the table for meals. It jumped upon her knee when she sat by the fire. It was her constant companion everywhere.

There was only one time when the kitten and Rosalie were separated and that was when she went to act in the theater in the town. Then it would scamper downstairs after her, as she went to the cab in her white dress. It would watch her drive away, and wander restlessly about the house, crying until she returned.

Rosalie had to go to the theater night after night with her father. The lady of the house, who was an actress in the same theater, went with them. She was not unkind to Rosalie, but simply took no notice of her. But to Rosalie's father she was *very* polite. She always gave him the best armchair in the parlor, and the chief place at the table, and cared for his comfort in every way. Often when Rosalie came suddenly into the room, she found her father and the lady of the house in deep conversation, which always stopped the moment she entered. As they drove together in the cab to the theater, many whispered words passed between them, of which Rosalie heard enough to make her feel quite sure that her father and the lady of the house were the best of friends.

So the weeks passed by, and the time drew near when the days would be long and light again, and her father's engagement at the theater would end, and he would set out on his summer rounds to all the fairs in the country. Rosalie was eagerly looking forward to this time. She was longing to get out of this dark lodging house; to have her own caravan to herself; to breathe once more the pure country air; to see the flowers, and the birds, and the trees again; and to see Toby, and to continue his reading lessons. To all this Rosalie looked forward with pleasure.

But Betsey Ann was sorry as the time drew near.

"La!" she would say, again and again, "whatever shall I do without you? Whoever shall I find to read to me then?"

And the clattery, old shoes dragged more heavily at the

thought, and the eyes of Betsey Ann filled with tears.

Yet she now knew for certain that the Good Shepherd loved her, and He would be with her even when Rosalie went away.

CHAPTER 16

A Dark Time

ONE morning, when Rosalie was upstairs in her attic room reading quietly to herself, the door opened softly. Betsey Ann came in with a very troubled look on her face, and sat down on one of the boxes.

"What's the matter, Betsey Ann?" asked Rosalie.

"Dear me, dear me!" said the kitchen maid. "I'm real sorry, that I am!"

"What *is* it?" asked Rosalie anxiously.

"If only it wasn't *her*, I shouldn't have minded so much," explained Betsey Ann. "But she is—, I can't tell you *what* she is. She's dreadful, sometimes. Oh dear, I *am* in a way about it!"

"About *what?*" asked Rosalie again.

"I've guessed as much a long time," said Betsey Ann, "but

141

I couldn't be quite sure. There's no mistake about it *now,* more's the pity!"

"Do tell me, please, Betsey Ann!" pleaded Rosalie.

"Well," said the girl, "I may as well tell you at once. You're going to have a new ma!"

"A what?" asked Rosalie.

"A ma; a new mother. *She's* going to be Mrs. Augustus Joyce."

"Oh, Betsey Ann!" said Rosalie in dismay. "Are you *sure?"*

"Yes!" said the girl. "Only *too* sure! One of the lodgers told me. And what's more, those two have gone off in a cab together just now. It's my belief they've gone to church to settle it. Ay! but I am sorry!"

"Oh, Betsey Ann!" Rosalie cried out in alarm. "What *shall* I do?"

"I never was so cut up about anything," said the maid. "She's been decent to you till now; but when she's married to your papa, she'll be another woman; you'll see! Oh dear— oh dear! But I must be off; I've lots to do afore she comes back, and I shall catch it if I waste my time. Oh, Rosalie! I wish I hadn't told you," she added as she saw the tears in Rosalie's eyes.

"Oh, it's better I should know," said Rosalie. "Thank you, dear Betsey Ann!"

"I'm real sorry, I am!" said the girl to herself as she went downstairs. "I'm a strong thing, but she's so young yet. I'm real sorry, I am!"

When Betsey Ann was gone, Rosalie was left to her own silent thoughts. All her dreams of quiet and peace in the caravan were at an end. They would either remain in the large lodging house or, if they went on their travels, the lady of the house would be also the lady of the caravan. And how would she ever be able to keep her locket and her letter to Aunt Lucy safe from those inquisitive eyes?

What a wretched life seemed ahead as she thought of the future! She seemed further from her Aunt Lucy than ever before. And how would she ever be able to read her Bible and pray, and learn more and more about the Good Shepherd?

Life suddenly seemed very dark and cheerless to Rosalie. The sunshine had faded from her sky, and all was chill and lifeless. She lost hope and she lost faith for a few minutes. She thought the Good Shepherd must have forgotten all about her, to let this new trouble come.

When she had cried for some time, and was becoming more and more miserable every moment, she stretched out her hand for her Bible, to see if she could find anything there to comfort her. She was turning quickly over the pages, not knowing exactly where to read, when the word *sheep* attracted her attention.

Ever since the old man had given her the picture at the fair, she always loved those texts which spoke of Jesus as the Shepherd, and His children as the sheep.

"My sheep hear My voice, and I know them, and they follow Me: and I give unto them eternal life; and they shall never perish, neither shall any man pluck them out of My hand."

The words seemed to soothe and comfort Rosalie, even before she had thought much about them. But when she began to think the verses over word by word, they seemed to Rosalie to be everything she wanted just then.

" 'My sheep.' It's the Good Shepherd speaking," thought Rosalie, "speaking about His sheep. *'My* sheep' He calls them. Am *I* one of them? Yes, I am. I *have* asked the Good Shepherd to find me, and I'm sure He has.

" 'My sheep hear My voice.' Please, Good Shepherd," said Rosalie, "may I hear *your* voice! May I do all that you tell me, and always try to please you!

" 'And I know them.' I'm glad the Good Shepherd knows *me*," thought Rosalie. "Because if He knows *me*, and knows all about me, then He knows just how worried I am. He knows all about father getting married, and the lady of the house coming to live in our caravan. Yes, He knows all that."

But the second verse seemed to Rosalie even more wonderful than the first: "I give unto them eternal life."

She knew what *eternal* meant; it meant forever and ever; her mother had taught her that. And this was the Shepherd's present to His sheep. Eternal life; they were to live in Heaven forever and ever. It was a wonderful thought. Rosalie's mind could not fully grasp it, but it did her good to think of it. It made present troubles and worries seem very small and insignificant. If she was going to live forever and ever, and ever, only a little bit of that long time would be spent in *this* sorrowful world! Oh, that was a very good thought. This sadness would not last always. Good times were coming, for Rosalie had received the Good Shepherd's present: *eternal life!*

" 'And they shall never perish, neither shall any man pluck them out of My hand.' After all," thought Rosalie, "this is the very best bit of all the text. I am one of the sheep, and I am in the Good Shepherd's hand. No one can take me out of it. What a strong hand He must have to hold all His sheep so tightly and securely."

"Good Shepherd," prayed Rosalie, "hold me tight. Don't

let anyone pluck me out of your hand; not father, not his new wife, nor any of the people here. Please hold me *very* tight. I am so afraid. I'm only a small sheep, and I have no one to help me, so please hold me tighter than the rest. Amen."

Rosalie rose from her knees very much at peace. Safe in the Good Shepherd's hand, who or what could harm her?

It was well she had been thus strengthened and comforted, for a few minutes afterwards she heard her father's voice calling her and, going downstairs, she found him sitting in the parlor with the lady of the house.

"Rosalie," said her father, with a theatrical bow, "allow me to introduce you to your lady mother!"

He evidently expected her to be very much astonished. Rosalie tried to smile, and went over to the lady of the house. And, as she put her hand in that of her new mother, it seemed to Rosalie as if the Good Shepherd tightened the hold of *His* hand on her!

Her father, after a few remarks about Rosalie having a mother again, dismissed her, and she went back to her attic room.

The very next day Rosalie saw clearly that Betsey Ann's predictions were likely to be fulfilled.

"Rosalie," said her stepmother, as soon as she came downstairs, "I intend that you shall make yourself useful now. I'm not going to have a daughter of mine idling away her time as you have been doing lately. Fetch some water and scour the sitting-room floor. And when you've done that, there's plenty more for you to do! *I* know how to make girls work!"

Rosalie could very easily believe that. Her father was standing by, and only laughed at what his new wife said.

"It will do her good," Rosalie heard him say, as she went out of the room. "You're quite right. She wants a bit of hard work!"

And a bit of hard work Rosalie certainly had. It was difficult to say whether she or Betsey Ann had more to do. Perhaps Rosalie's life was the harder one, for after working all day, she had to go to the theater and take her part in the play. When she came home at night she was so worn out she could hardly drag herself up to the attic to bed.

The hard work was not what Rosalie minded most. There was fault finding from morning till night, without one single word of praise and encouragement. There were unkind, cruel words, and even blows to bear. But what was worse than all these was that she had to wait upon many of the rude and noisy lodgers.

Would she really be kept safe in this dreadful place? Sometimes Rosalie felt as if she would sink under it; but the Good Shepherd's hand was around her. No one could pluck her out of *that* hand. No evil thing could touch her; the Good Shepherd's sheep was held tightly in His almighty grasp.

Rosalie saw very little of her father now. He was out nearly all the afternoon, only coming home in time to go with them to the theater at night. Then, when the performance was over, he often did not go home with his wife and Rosalie, but sent them off in a cab, and went drinking with his friends.

Rosalie never knew when her father returned home. He had a latchkey, and let himself in after all in the house were asleep. Rosalie would not see him until dinnertime the next day, when he would come downstairs in a very bad temper.

She was often unhappy about him, and would have done

anything she could to make him think about God.

But it seemed no use to speak to him. The Good Shepherd longed to find him; but he refused to hear His voice. He had hardened his heart, and, for the last time, had turned away from the love of God.

One night, when Rosalie had gone to bed with the kitten beside her on the pillow, and had fallen asleep from weariness and exhaustion, she was startled by a hand on her shoulder, and heard Betsey Ann's voice saying, "Rosalie, Rosalie! What can it be?"

She started quickly, and saw Betsey Ann standing beside her, looking very frightened.

"Rosalie," she said, "didn't you hear it?"

"Hear what?" asked Rosalie.

"Why, I was fast asleep," said Betsey Ann, "and I woke in an instant, and I heard the doorbell ring."

"Are you sure?" said Rosalie. "I heard nothing."

"No," said Betsey Ann; "and missis doesn't seem to have heard neither. Everyone's been asleep a long time. But then, you see, I have to go so quickly to open it when that bell rings in the day, I expect the sound of it would make me jump up if I was *ever* so fast asleep."

"Are you quite sure, Betsey Ann?" asked Rosalie once more.

But she had hardly spoken the words before the bell was pulled again, very loudly, and left no doubt about it.

"Do you mind coming with me, Rosalie?" asked Betsey Ann, as she prepared to go downstairs.

"No, not at all," said Rosalie. "I'm not afraid."

So the two girls hastily put on their clothes and went downstairs. Just as they arrived at the bottom of the steep staircase the bell rang again, louder than before, and the lady of the house came on the landing to see who it was.

"Please, ma'am," said Betsey Ann, "it's the house bell. Me and Rosalie are just going to open the door."

"Oh! it's nothing, I should think," said she. "It will be someone who has arrived by the train, and has come to the wrong door."

Whilst they were talking the bell rang again, more violently than before, and Betsey Ann opened the door. It was a dark night, but she could see a man standing on the doorstep.

"Is this Mrs. Joyce's?" he inquired.

"Yes," said the maid. "She lives here."

"She's wanted," said the man. "Tell her to be quick and come."

"What's the matter?" asked Rosalie.

"It's an accident," said the man. "He's in the hospital, is her husband. He's been run over by a cab. I'll take her there if she'll be quick. I'm a mate of Joyce's."

Rosalie stood as if she had been stunned, unable to speak or move, whilst Betsey Ann went upstairs to tell her mistress.

"It's all that drink," said the man, talking more to himself than to Rosalie. "He never saw the cab, nor heard it. He stepped right under the wheels. I was passing by, I was, and I said to myself, 'That's Joyce.' So I followed to the hospital, and came to tell his wife. Dear me, it's a bad job, it is!"

In a few minutes, Mrs. Augustus Joyce came downstairs, dressed to go out. Rosalie ran up to her and begged to go with her, but was ordered to go back to bed, and her stepmother hastened out with the man.

Rosalie longed for morning to dawn. She lay awake all night, straining her ears for any sound which might tell her that her stepmother had returned.

At length, as the grey morning light was stealing into the room, the doorbell rang again, and Betsey Ann went to open the door for her mistress. Rosalie did not dare to go downstairs to hear what had happened.

Presently, the clattering shoes slowly came upstairs, and Betsey Ann came into the attic.

"Tell me," said Rosalie. "What is it?"

"He's dead," said Betsey Ann quietly. "He was dead when she got there. He never knew nothing after the wheels went over him. Isn't it awful, though?"

Rosalie could not speak and could not cry. She sat quite still and motionless, and knew that if her father had never let the Good Shepherd find him, it was now too late.

CHAPTER 17

Running Away

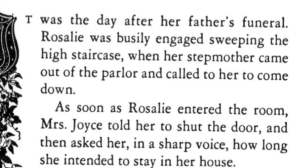

T was the day after her father's funeral. Rosalie was busily engaged sweeping the high staircase, when her stepmother came out of the parlor and called to her to come down.

As soon as Rosalie entered the room, Mrs. Joyce told her to shut the door, and then asked her, in a sharp voice, how long she intended to stay in her house.

"I don't know," said Rosalie, timidly.

"Then you *ought* to know!" returned Mrs. Joyce. "I suppose you don't expect *me* to keep *you* and do for you! You're nothing to *me*, you know!"

"No," said Rosalie. "I know I'm not."

"So I thought I'd better tell you at once," she said, "that you might know what to expect. I'm going to speak to the workhouse about you. That's the best place for you now. *They'll* make you like hard work, and get a good place for you, like Betsey Ann."

"Oh, no!" said Rosalie, quickly. "No, I don't want to go *there!*"

"Don't *want?*" repeated Mrs. Joyce. "I dare say you *don't* want; but beggars can't be choosers, you know. If you'd been a nice, smart, strong girl, I might have kept you instead of Betsey Ann. But a little thing like you wouldn't be worth her salt. No, no, miss; your fine days are over. To the workhouse you'll go, as sure as I'm alive."

"Please," began Rosalie, "my mother had some relatives—"

"Rubbish, child!" said her stepmother, interrupting her. "*I* never heard of your mother having any relatives. I don't believe she had any, of if she had, they're not likely to have anything to say to you. No, no; the workhouse is the place for you, and I shall make sure you go to it before you're a day older. Be off now, and finish the stairs."

"Betsey Ann," said Rosalie, when they were upstairs together that night, long after everyone else in that large house was fast asleep. "Betsey Ann, dear Betsey Ann, I'm going away!"

"La! bless me!" said Betsey Ann. "What do you say?"

"I'm going away tomorrow," whispered Rosalie. "Come into my room, and I'll tell you all about it."

The two girls sat down on the mattress and Rosalie told Betsey Ann what her stepmother had said to her. Rosalie said she could not bear to go to the workhouse, and had made up her mind to leave the lodging house before breakfast the next morning and *never* come back!

"But, Rosalie," said Betsey Ann, "whatever will you *do?*

You can't live on air, child. You'll *die* if you go away like that!"

"Look here," said Rosalie, in a very low whisper, "I can trust you, Betsey Ann, and I'll show you something."

She brought out the small parcel from beneath her dress. When she had opened it, she handed the locket to Betsey Ann.

"La, how beautiful!" said the girl. "I never saw it before."

"No," explained Rosalie. "I promised my mother I would never lose it; and I've been so afraid that someone would see it, and take it from me."

"Whoever is this pretty young lady, Rosalie?"

"She's my mother's sister. That is her picture when she was quite young. She is married now, and has a girl of her own. I'll tell you all about it," said Rosalie. "Just before my mother died, she gave me that locket, and she said if I ever had the chance, I was to go to my Aunt Lucy. She wrote a letter for me to take, to say who I am and to ask my Aunt Lucy to be kind to me.

"Here's the letter," said Rosalie, taking it out of the parcel. "That's my mother's writing.

" 'MRS. LESLIE,

" 'Melton Parsonage.'

"Didn't she write beautifully?" said Rosalie proudly, showing the envelope to her friend.

"Well, Rosalie," said Betsey Ann, "what do you mean to do?"

"I mean to go to my Aunt Lucy and give her the letter."

"*She'll* never let you go, Rosalie. It's no use trying. She said you have to go to the workhouse, and she'll keep her word!"

"Yes, I know she'll never *let* me go," said Rosalie. "So I'm leaving tomorrow morning before breakfast. She doesn't get up till eleven, and I shall be far away by then."

"But, Rosalie, do you know your way?"

"No. I shall have to ask, I suppose. How far is Pendleton from here, Betsey Ann? Do you know?"

"Yes," said Betsey Ann. "There was a woman in the workhouse came from there. She often told us how she walked the distance on a cold, snowy day. It's fourteen or fifteen miles, I think. But why Pendleton?"

"Well, that's the town where the old man gave me my picture," said Rosalie. "It was the first village we passed through after that, where my Aunt Lucy lived. Melton must be about five miles further than Pendleton."

"Oh, Rosalie!" said Betsey Ann. "That's nearly twenty miles! You'll never be able to walk all *that* way!"

"Oh, yes," insisted Rosalie. "I must try, because once I get there—oh, Betsey Ann, just think, once I get there, to my own dear Aunt Lucy . . . why, what is the matter?"

Betsey Ann buried her face in her hands, and began to sob.

"La, bless you, it's all right!" she said, as Rosalie tried to comfort her. "You'll be happy there, and it will be all right. But, oh dear me, to think I've to stay here without you!"

"Poor Betsey Ann!" said Rosalie, as she laid her hand on the girl's rough hair. "What can I do?"

"Oh, it's all right, Rosalie. It's better than seeing you go to the workhouse. But I didn't think it would come so *soon*. Can't you tell the Good Shepherd, Rosalie, and ask Him to look after *me* a bit, when you're gone?"

"Yes," said Rosalie. "Let us tell Him now."

So they knelt down, hand in hand, on the attic floor, and

Rosalie prayed, "Good Shepherd, I am going away. Please take care of Betsey Ann, and comfort her, and help her to do right, and never let her feel lonely or unhappy. And please take care of me, and bring me safe to my Aunt Lucy. And if Betsey Ann and I never meet again in this world, please may we neet in Heaven! Amen."

Then they rose from their knees, in tears and smiles, and began to make preparations for Rosalie's departure.

Rosalie decided she would take very little with her, for she had so far to walk that she could not carry much. She filled a small bag with the things that she needed most. Then she wrapped her small Bible up, and put it in the middle with the small pair of blue shoes which had belonged to the little brother she had never known. Her picture, too, was not forgotten, nor was the card with the hymn printed on it. When all was ready, they went to bed: but neither of them could sleep much that night.

As soon as it was light, Rosalie wrapped herself in her mother's warm shawl, for it was a raw, chilly morning, and took her bag in her hand. Then she went into Betsey Ann's attic room to say goodbye.

"What am I to tell the missis, when she asks where you've gone?" said the distressed maid.

"You can say that I've gone to my mother's relatives, and am not coming back. She won't ask any more, if you say that. She'll only be too glad to get rid of me! But I'd rather she didn't know where my Aunt Lucy lives, so don't say anything about that, please, Betsey Ann."

The girl promised, and then with many tears they took leave of each other.

Betsey Ann was opening the door for Rosalie, when she caught sight of something very black and soft under

Rosalie's large shawl.

"La, bless me!" she cried. "What's that?"

"It's only the poor kitten," said Rosalie. "I couldn't leave her behind. She took a piece of fish the other day, and the mistress was so angry she is going to give her poison. She said last night she would poison my kitten today. She said, 'Two pieces of rubbish got rid of in one day: tomorrow, *you* shall go to the workhouse, and that wretched little thief of a kitten shall be poisoned.' And then she laughed, Betsey Ann. So I couldn't leave my kitten behind, could I?" and Rosalie stroked its black fur as she spoke.

"But how will you carry it, Rosalie? It won't be good all that way, rolled up like that."

"Oh, I shall manage. It will walk a bit when we get in the country. It follows me just like a dog."

"And what are you going to eat on the way, Rosalie? Let me fetch something out of the pantry for you."

"Oh no!" said Rosalie, decidedly. "I won't take anything, because it isn't mine. But I have a piece of bread that I saved from breakfast, and I have twopence which my father gave me once, so I shall manage till I get there."

Then Rosalie was out in the great world, and Betsey Ann stood at the door to watch her go down the street. Over and over again Rosalie came back to say goodbye, over and over again she turned round to wave to the servant girl, who was watching her. And then, when she turned the corner and could no longer see Betsey Ann's friendly face, Rosalie felt really alone.

The streets looked very wide and unfriendly, and Rosalie knew she was unprepared. She had no one to take care of her. Then she looked up to the blue sky, and asked the Good Shepherd to help her, and to bring her safely to her journey's end.

It was about six o'clock when Rosalie started out that morning. Some men were going to work, hurrying quickly past her. Rosalie did not like to stop any of them to ask the way. They seemed too busy to have time to speak to her. She ventured to put the question to a boy who was sauntering along, whistling, with his hands in his pockets. But he only laughed, and asked her why she wanted to know. So Rosalie walked on, very much afraid that she might be walking in the wrong direction after all. Next, she asked some children on a doorstep, but they were frightened at being spoken to, and ran indoors.

Rosalie went up to an old woman who was opening her shutters, and asked her if she would be so very good as to tell her the way to Pendleton.

"What, my dear?" said the old woman. "Speak up, I'm deaf!"

But though Rosalie shouted again and again, she could not make the old woman hear, and at last had to give it up, and go on her way. She was feeling very lonely, not knowing which way to turn, or to whom to go for help. True, there were many people in the street, but they were walking quickly along, and Rosalie was afraid to stop them. She had come some way from the street in which she had lived with her stepmother, and had never been in this part of the large town before. She was feeling very hungry, for she had not dared to eat any breakfast. She did not like to eat her one piece of bread, for she would need it later in the day. She broke off a small piece, and gave it to the hungry kitten which was mewing under her shawl.

"Oh," thought Rosalie, "if I only had someone to help me just now—someone to show where to go, and what to do!"

There was a story which Rosalie once read in her Bible. This suddenly came into her mind. It was a story of Jesus when He was on earth. The story told how He sent two of His disciples into the city of Jerusalem to find a place for Him and for themselves, where they could eat the Passover. The two men did not know to which house to go. They did not know who, in the great city of Jerusalem, would be willing to give a room. But Jesus told them that as soon as they came inside the city gate they would see a man walking, carrying a pitcher of water. When they saw this man, they were to follow him, and go down just the same streets he did. Jesus told them the man would go into a house, and that would be the house in which they were to eat the Passover.

Rosalie remembered this story now as she stood at the corner of a street, not knowing which way to turn. How she wished that a man with a pitcher of water would appear, and walk in front of her!

But though she looked up and down the street, she saw no one at all like the man in the story. There were plenty of men, but none of them had pitchers, nor did they seem at all likely to guide her to the right way!

But Jesus, the Good Shepherd, was the same, Rosalie thought; as kind now as He was then. So she spoke to Him in her heart. "Good Shepherd, *please* send me a man with a pitcher of water to show me the way, for I am very frightened, and I don't know what to do. Please, Jesus. Amen."

CHAPTER 18

The Pitcher

OSALIE had shut her eyes as she said her prayer. When she opened them she saw before her a little girl about five years old, in a very clean print frock and white pinafore, with a small earthenware pitcher in her hand. Rosalie almost felt as if she had fallen from Heaven! This girl was not a man, to be sure, and the pitcher was full of milk, not water. Yet it seemed very strange that she should appear just then.

The small girl was gazing up into Rosalie's face and wondering why she was shutting her eyes. As soon as Rosalie opened them she said, "Please will you open our shop door for me? I'm afraid of spilling the milk."

Rosalie turned round, and behind where she was standing

158

was a small shop. In the window were children's slates and slate pencils, with colored paper twisted round them, and a few wooden tops, and balls of string, and little boxes of ninepins, and a basket full of marbles, and pink and blue shuttlecocks. It was a very quiet shop indeed, and it looked as if very few customers ever entered it. The slate pencils and battledores and marbles looked as if they had stood in exactly the same places since long before the girl was born.

Rosalie lifted the latch and opened the door of the small shop for the child to go in. And the pitcher went in with her.

Rosalie felt she must follow, and that here she would surely find someone to tell her the way.

"Popsey," called a voice from the next room, "is that you?"

"Yes, grannie," said the child, "and I've not spilt a drop—not one single drop—grannie."

"What a good little Popsey!" said her grannie, coming out of the back parlor to take the milk from the child's hands.

"Please, ma'am," said Rosalie, seizing the opportunity, "would you be so very kind as to tell me the way to Pendleton?"

"Yes, to be sure," said the old woman. "Take the first turn to the right, and you'll find yourself on the Pendleton road."

"Oh, thank you very much," said Rosalie. "Is it a very long way to Pendleton, please?"

"Ay, my dear," said the old woman. "It's a good, long step—Popsey, take the milk in to grandfather, he's waiting breakfast—it's a good, long way to Pendleton, my dear, maybe fourteen or fifteen miles."

"Oh dear! that sounds a very *long* way!" said Rosalie.

"Who wants to go there, my dear?" asked the old woman.

"I want to go," said Rosalie.

"You want to go, child! Why, who are you going with? And how are you going? You're surely not going to *walk?"*

"Yes, I am," said Rosalie. "Thank you, ma'am. I must walk as fast as I can."

"Why, you don't look fit to go, I'm sure," said the old woman. "Whatever is your mother about, to let you go?"

"I haven't got a mother!" said Rosalie, bursting into tears. "She's dead. I haven't got a mother any more."

"Don't cry, my poor lamb!" said the old woman, wiping Rosalie's eyes with her apron. "Popsey hasn't got a mother neither. Her mother's dead—she lives with us, does Popsey. Maybe your grandmother lives in Pendleton. Does she?"

"No," said Rosalie. "I'm going to my mother's sister, who lives in a village near Pendleton. I was to have gone to the workhouse today, but I think, perhaps, she'll take care of me, if I can only get there."

"Poor lamb!" said the old woman. "What a way you have to go! Have you had your breakfast yet? You look fit to faint!"

"No," said Rosalie. "I have a piece of bread in my bag, but I was keeping it till I got out of town."

"Jonathan," called out the old woman, "come here."

Rosalie could hear a chair being pushed from the table on the stone floor in the kitchen, and the next moment an old man came into the shop, with spectacles on his nose, a blue handkerchief tied round his neck, and a black velvet waistcoat.

"Look ye here, Jonathan," said his wife, "did you ever hear the like? Here's this poor lamb going to walk all the way to Pendleton, and never had a bite of nothing all this blessed day! What do you say to that, Jonathan?"

The Pitcher

"I say," said the old man, "that breakfast's all ready, and the coffee will be cold."

"Yes; so do I, Jonathan," said the old woman. "So come along, child, and have a sup before you start."

The next minute Rosalie was seated by the round table in the back kitchen with a cup of steaming coffee and a slice of hot bread before her. Such a cozy kitchen it was, with a bright fire burning in the grate, and another hot loaf standing on the top of the oven. The fire irons shone like silver, and everything in the room was as neat and clean and bright as it was possible for them to be.

Popsey was sitting on a chair between the old man and woman, and the pitcher of milk was just in front of her. She had been pouring some of it into her grandfather's coffee.

The old man was very attentive to Rosalie, and wanted her to eat some of everything on the table. But before Rosalie would eat a morsel herself she said, looking into the old woman's face, "Please, ma'am, may my kitten have something to eat? It's so very, very hungry."

"Your kitten!" exclaimed the old woman. "Why, what do you mean, child? Where is it?"

But the kitten answered this question by peeping out from Rosalie's shawl. All were astonished to see it; but when Rosalie told its story, and the old woman heard that it was motherless—like Popsey—it received a warm welcome. The pitcher of milk was emptied for the hungry kitten, and when its breakfast was over it sat purring in front of the bright fire.

Popsey ran to the kitchen and climbed on a chair to fetch a jar of jam. Rosalie thought she had never tasted such good bread, nor drank such delicious coffee. Popsey was delighted with the kitten, and wanted to give it all her breakfast.

Popsey ran to the kitchen . . .

When breakfast was over Popsey got down from her chair and went to a chest of drawers, which stood in a corner near the fireplace. It was a very old-fashioned chest of drawers, and on the top of it were arranged some equally old-fashioned books. In the middle of these was a large, well-worn family Bible.

Popsey put a chair against the chest of drawers and, standing on tiptoe on it, brought down the Bible from its place. It was almost as much as she could lift, but she put both her arms round it and carried it to her grandfather. The old man cleared a space for it on the table, and laid it before him.

Then there was a pause, in which the old man took an extra pair of spectacles from a leather case, fixed them on his nose, and turned over the leaves of his Bible. Then, when he had found his place, he began to read a psalm. The psalm might have been chosen on purpose for Rosalie, for it said, "The Lord is my shepherd: I shall not want."

That was the first verse of the psalm; and it went on to tell how the Good Shepherd leads His sheep into green pastures, and makes them to lie down beside still waters: and how the sheep need fear no evil, for He is with them. His rod and staff comfort them.

Then, when he had finished reading, the old man said a prayer, in which Rosalie and Popsey were both named and committed to the Good Shepherd's care.

Rosalie felt it was high time she should go on her journey. But the old woman would not hear of her going till she had wrapped up some cake, in a parcel, and slipped it into Rosalie's bag. After this, all three—the old man, the old woman, and Popsey—went to the door to see Rosalie on her way.

The Pitcher

Popsey could hardly tear herself from the kitten, and the old woman could not make up her mind to let go of Rosalie. But at length the goodbyes were over, and Rosalie set off once more on her travels, feeling warmed and comforted and strengthened.

It was about eight o'clock now, so there was no time to lose. She easily found Pendleton Road, and went as the old woman had directed her to. She would pass through several villages, the old woman said, but she was not to turn aside in any direction. So Rosalie had no further anxiety about the way she was to go. All she had to do was to walk along as quickly as possible.

The first part of the road lay through the outskirts of the town. On either side of the way were rows of red-brick houses and small shops, and every now and then a patch of field or garden.

By degrees the houses and shops became fewer, and the patches of field and garden became more numerous. Then the houses disappeared altogether, and there was nothing on either side of the road but fields and gardens.

The sun was shining, and the hedges were covered with wild roses. The day was becoming warmer. Over Rosalie's head there was a lark singing in midair, and by the side of the path grew the small, pink flowers of the wild convolvulus. Rosalie could not help stopping to gather some sprays from this, and to twist them round her hat. It was many months since she had seen flowers. They brought the old days back to her, when Toby used to put her down from the caravan so that she could gather flowers for her mother.

For the first few miles Rosalie enjoyed her walk. Everything was so bright and pleasant. Sometimes she put

A rest by the wayside.

the kitten on the ground, and it ran by her side.

At last, Rosalie sat on a bank and ate the cake which Popsey's grandmother had given her. And the little black kitten had its fair share!

As the day went on, the kitten became tired, and would walk no more. Rosalie grew tired also. Her feet went slowly, and she was worried that night would come on long before she reached Pendleton. The sun was hidden by clouds, and the wind began to sweep through the trees, blowing against Rosalie, so that she could hardly make any way against it.

Then came the rain. Only a few drops at first, then quicker and quicker. Rosalie's shawl became wet through. Her clothes clung heavily to her ankles. But on she walked, very heavily and wearily, and the rain poured down, and the kitten shivered under the shawl. Rosalie did her very best to keep it warm, and every now and then she stroked its wet fur, and spoke a word of comfort to it.

Wearily, Rosalie pressed on, as she struggled against the cold and piercing wind.

Would she ever reach the town? Would she ever hold on till she arrived at her Aunt Lucy's? Doubts entered Rosalie's mind for the first time.

CHAPTER 19

Skirrywinks

OSALIE was almost ready to give up and sit down by the roadside, when she heard a sound behind her. It was the rumbling of wheels, and in another minute Rosalie saw two large caravans, very much like the caravan in which she used to travel with her mother. She felt as if she were dreaming as she looked at them.

The caravans were painted a brilliant yellow, just as her father's caravans had been. There were muslin curtains and pink bows in the windows, just like those through which she had so often peeped.

When the caravans came up to Rosalie, she saw a woman standing at the door of the first one, and talking to the man who was driving.

The woman caught sight of Rosalie.

"Holloa!" she called out. "Where are you off to?"

"Please," said Rosalie. "I'm going to Pendleton, if only I can get there."

"Give her a lift, Thomas," said the woman. "Give the child a lift. It's an awful day to be struggling along against wind and storm."

"All right," said Thomas, pulling up. "I've no objections, if the lass likes to get in."

Rosalie was grateful indeed for this offer, and climbed into the caravan, which started off again at once. The woman opened the door for her, and took off her wet shawl as she went in.

"Why! you've got a kitten there," she said as she did so. "Wherever are you taking it to? It's half drowned with the rain!"

"Yes, poor kitten!" said Rosalie. "I must try to dry it—it's so cold!"

"Well, I'll make a place for both of you near the fire," said the woman, "if only my children will get out of the way."

Rosalie looked in vain for any children in the moving caravan; but the woman pointed to a large black dog, a pigeon, and a kitten, which were sitting together on the floor.

"Come, Skirrywinks," said the woman, addressing herself to her kitten. "Come to me."

As soon as she said, "Skirrywinks," the kitten—who had appeared to be asleep before—lifted up her head and jumped on the woman's knee. The great, black dog was ordered to the other end of the caravan, and the pigeon perched upon the dog's head.

The woman gave Rosalie a seat near the stove, where she warmed her hands and dried and comforted her own kitten.

No words could tell how thankful she was for this help on her way. She felt sure that Thomas must be a man with a pitcher of water, sent to help her on her journey!

For some time the woman leaned out of the caravan, continuing her conversation with her husband, and Rosalie was able to look about her. The inside of the caravan was very like that in which she had been born and lived for so many years. There was a small cooking stove, just like that which her mother had used. In the corner was a large cupboard, filled with cups and saucers and plates, just like the one which Rosalie herself had arranged so often. But what caught her eye more than anything else was that on the side of the caravan was pinned her picture—the picture of the Good Shepherd and the sheep!

It was exactly the same picture, and the same text was underneath it.

"Rejoice with me; for I have found my sheep which was lost. There is joy in the presence of the angels of God over one sinner that repenteth."

Rosalie could not help feeling in her bag to be sure that her own picture was safe, in case this was *her* picture!

The picture seemed to have hung there for some time though, for it was very smoky and discolored. But still it looked good, Rosalie thought, and her eyes filled with tears as she gazed at it. It brought her mother's dream to her mind, and carried her thoughts away from the caravan to the home above where even now, perhaps, her mother was being called by the Good Shepherd to rejoice with Him over some sheep which was lost, but which the Good Shepherd had found!

The woman began to talk to Rosalie, to ask her where she had come from, where she was going, and what she was going to do. She seemed friendly, though she spoke with a rough voice. All the time she was talking, Skirrywinks, the kitten, was sitting on her shoulder. And the pigeon was now on her head. Rosalie's kitten seemed afraid of the large, black dog, and crept into her mistress's arms.

When they had chatted together for some time, Rosalie mentioned the picture, saying that it seemed so strange to see it here, for she had one exactly like it.

"Oh! have you?" said the woman. "That Jinx's picture. An old man gave it to him—just a year ago, it will be. It was at a Pendleton fair."

"Why, that's where I got mine!" said Rosalie. "It must be the same old man."

"I expect it was," said the woman. "He came to all the caravans on a Sunday afternoon."

"Oh yes, it's the same old man," said Rosalie. "I have *my* picture here, in my bag. I wouldn't *ever* part with it!"

"Wouldn't you?" said the woman, sounding surprised. "Well, I don't believe Jinx would, either. He pinned it up that very Sunday, and it's been there ever since."

"Who's Jinx?" asked Rosalie, excited at the thought of sharing her love of Jesus with someone else.

"He's our boy. At least, he lives with us. Me and Thomas haven't got any children of our own, so we keeps a few. There's Jinx, he's chief of them; and then there's Skirrywinks, and Tozer, and Spanco, and then there's Jeremiah—you haven't seen Jeremiah, he's in bed. You'll see him when Jinx comes."

"Where *is* Jinx?" asked Rosalie, almost expecting he would turn out to be yet another animal, hidden away in a corner of the caravan.

"Oh, he's in the next van, with Lord Fatimore," said the

woman. "He'll be here soon, when it's time for these young people to be fed and trained. He's very clever, is Jinx. You never saw anyone so clever in all your life. I'll be bound he can make 'em do *anything!* We might just as well shut up, if we hadn't Jinx. His act is a great deal more popular than Lord Fatimore's is—folks say they never saw such a sight as when Jeremiah and Skirrywinks dance the polka together; and it's Jinx that has taught them."

In about half an hour the caravans were stopped, and the wonderful Jinx arrived. He was short, no taller than Rosalie. He was very hump-backed, with a wizened and careworn face. It was hard to tell whether he was a man or a boy.

"Jinx," said the woman as he entered, "here's a young lady come to see your performance."

"Most happy, miss," said Jinx, with a bow.

The moment that he came into the caravan, Skirrywinks and the dog sat on their hind legs, and the pigeon flew to his head. As soon as he spoke, Rosalie heard a noise in a basket behind her as of something struggling to get out.

"I hear you, Jeremiah," said Jinx. "You shall come, you shall."

He took the basket, and put his hand inside.

"Now, Jeremiah," he said. "Come out, and show the company how you put on your new coat."

Out of the basket he brought a hare, which was extremely tame and allowed itself to be dressed in a scarlet jacket.

Then Jinx made all the animals go through their different acts, after which each received its share of food. But Skirrywinks, the kitten, seemed to be Jinx's favorite. Long after the others were dismissed she sat on his shoulders, watching his every movement.

"Well, what do you think of them?" he asked, turning to

Rosalie when he had finished.

"They're very clever," she said. "Very clever, indeed!"

"That kitten of yours couldn't do as much," said Jinx, looking scornfully at the kitten which lay in Rosalie's lap.

"No," said Rosalie. "But she's a very precious kitten, even though she doesn't jump through rings nor dance polkas."

"Well, tastes differ," said Jinx. "I prefer Skirrywinks."

"You've got a picture like mine," said Rosalie, after a time.

"Oh," he said. "Have you one like it? I got it at Pendleton fair."

"And so did I," said Rosalie. "The same old man gave one to me." There was a pause. Then Rosalie asked, "Has *He* found *you*, Mr. Jinx?" in a quiet voice.

"Has *who* found me? What do you mean?" said Jinx, with a laugh.

"Why, haven't you read the story in the picture?" asked Rosalie. "It says where it is underneath." A great feeling of disappointment swept over her.

"No, not I," said Jinx, laughing again. "Thinks I, when the old man gave it to me, it's a pretty picture, and I'll stick it on the wall. But I've never troubled my head anymore about it."

"Oh, my mother and I—we used to read it nearly every day," said Rosalie. "It's a good story!" She tried not to let her disappointment show in her voice.

"Is it?" said Jinx. "I should like to hear it. Tell it to me now, please. It will pass the time as we go along."

"I can read it, if you like," said Rosalie. "I have it here."

"All right! Read on," said Jinx, earnestly.

Rosalie took a Bible from her bag. But before she began to read, Jinx called out to the woman who was leaning out of the caravan, and talking to her husband.

"Old mother!" he called out. "Come and hear the little 'un read. She's going to give us the history of that there picture of mine. You know nothing about it, I'll be bound!"

But Jinx was wrong, for when Rosalie had finished reading, the woman said, "That will be the Bible you read out of. I've read that often when I was a girl. I went to a good Sunday school then."

"And don't you ever read it now?" asked Rosalie. Reading the Bible had become such a natural thing to her.

"Oh, I'm not so bad as you think," said the woman, not answering the question. "I think of all those things at times. I'm a decent woman, in my way. I know the Bible well enough, and there's a many a *deal worse* than I am!"

"If you would like," said Rosalie, "I'll find it for you in *your* Bible, and then you can read it again—as you used to do when you were a girl."

The woman hesitated when Rosalie said this.

"Well, to tell you the truth, I haven't got my Bible here," she said. "My husband sent all the things we wasn't wanting at the time to his relations in Scotland. Somehow the Bible got packed up in the trunk with all the other things. It will be a year since now. I was very vexed about it at the time."

"Has the Good Shepherd found you, ma'am?" asked Rosalie, as she had asked several people since finding Jesus herself.

"Oh, I don't know, child. I don't much want to be found. I'm not so bad as all that. I'm a very decent woman, I am. Thomas will tell you that."

"Then I suppose," said Rosalie, looking very puzzled, "you must be one of the ninety-and-nine."

"What do you mean, child?" asked the woman, in surprise.

173

"I mean, one of the ninety-nine sheep which don't need any repentance, because they were never lost. The Good Shepherd never found them, nor carried them home, nor said of them, 'Rejoice with me; for I have found my sheep which was lost.' "

"Well," said Jinx, looking at Rosalie with a half-amused face, "if the old mother's one of the ninety-nine, what am I?"

"I don't know," said Rosalie, with a thoughtful smile. "You must know better than I do, Mr. Jinx."

"Well, how is one to know?" he answered. "If I'm not one of the ninety-nine, what am I then?"

"Do you *really* want to know?" asked Rosalie. "Because if not, we won't talk about it, please."

"Yes," said Jinx, in quite a different tone. "I really do want to know about it."

Rosalie smiled a friendly smile at him. "My mother said one day she thought there were only three kinds of sheep. There are the ninety-nine sheep who were never lost, and who need no repentance because they've never done anything wrong nor said anything wrong, but have always been good, and holy, and pure. That's *one* kind. My mother said she thought the ninety-nine must be the angels; she didn't think there were any in *this* world!"

"Hear that, old mother?" said Jinx. "You must be an angel, you see! Well, little 'un, go on."

"And then there are the lost sheep," said Rosalie. "They're far away from the fold. They don't love the Good Shepherd, and sometimes they don't even know that they *are* lost. They are very far from the right way—very far from being perfectly good and holy."

"Well," said Jinx. "And what's the *third* kind of sheep?"

"Oh, that's the sheep which was lost, but is found again!"

"And what are *they* like?"

"They love the Good Shepherd. They listen to His voice, and follow Him, and never, never want to wander from the fold."

"Is that *all* the kinds?" asked Jinx.

"Yes," said Rosalie, "that's all."

"Well," said Jinx, thoughtfully. "I've made up my mind which I am."

"Which, Mr. Jinx?" asked Rosalie.

"Well, I can't be one of the ninety-nine, because I've done lots of bad things in my life. I've got into tempers, and I've sworn, and I've done heaps of bad things: so *that's* out of the question. And I can't be a *found* sheep, because I don't know the Good Shepherd—I never think about Him at all. So I suppose I'm a *lost* sheep. That's a very bad thing to be, isn't it?"

"Yes, very bad, if you are *always* a lost sheep," explained Rosalie. "But if you are one of the lost sheep, then *Jesus came to seek you* and to *save you.*"

"Didn't He come to seek and save the old mother?" asked Jinx.

"Not if she's one of the ninety-nine," said Rosalie. "It says, 'The Son of Man is come to seek and to save that which was *lost,*' so if she *isn't* lost, it doesn't mean her."

The woman looked very uncomfortable when Rosalie said this. She did not like to think that Jesus had not come to save her.

"Well, and suppose a fellow *knows* he's one of the lost sheep," asked Jinx. "What has he got to do?"

"He must call out to the Good Shepherd, and tell Him he's lost, and ask the Good Shepherd to find him."

"Well, but first of all, I suppose," said Jinx, "he must make himself a *bit ready* to go to the Good Shepherd—leave off a few of his bad ways, and make himself decent a bit."

"Oh, no!" said Rosalie. "He'd never get back to the fold *that* way! First of all, he must *tell* the Good Shepherd he's lost. Then the Shepherd, who has been seeking him for a long, long time, will find him at once, and carry him home on His shoulders. And *then* the Good Shepherd will help him to be better."

"Well, I'll think about what you've said," Jinx replied. "Thank you, little 'un."

The yellow caravans were drawn up by the roadside, and the woman took tea from the stove, and Jinx was sent to the next caravan with Lord Fatimore's food. Rosalie, offering to help, was sent after him with his pipe and tobacco.

She found Lord Fatimore sitting in state in his own caravan. He was an immensely fat man or, rather, an enormously overgrown youth. He was lounging in an easy chair, looking the picture of laziness. He brightened up a little as he saw his meal arriving—this was the great event of his day.

When Rosalie returned to the caravan the woman was alone, stroking Skirrywinks, who was lying on her knee. Her thoughts were far away.

"Child," she said to Rosalie. "I'm *not* one of the ninety-nine. I *do* need Jesus. I'm one of the *lost* sheep."

"I'm so glad," said Rosalie, "because the Good Shepherd is seeking you. Won't you ask Him to find you?"

But before she could answer, Thomas and Jinx came in for their tea, and they all insisted on Rosalie joining them.

After they had eaten, Thomas sat in the caravan and smoked his pipe, and Jinx drove. Rosalie sat still, thinking.

Skirrywinks

But she was so tired that after a little time the picture on the wall, Thomas, the woman, Skirrywinks, Tozer, and Spanco faded from her sight, and she fell asleep.

CHAPTER 20

Mother Manikin's Chairs

HEN Rosalie awoke it was almost dark. The woman was lighting the oil lamp, and filling the kettle from a large can of water.

"Where are we?" asked Rosalie sleepily.

"Close upon Pendleton, little 'un," answered Jinx. "Get up, and see the lights in the distance."

"Oh dear, and it's nearly dark!" said Rosalie.

"Never mind, my dear. We're almost there," said Thomas. He did not know that Rosalie had five more miles to walk to Melton.

The wheels of the caravan rumbled on and, in a quarter of an hour, they came into the streets of the town. It was quite dark now, the lamps were all lighted, and men were going

178

home from work.

When they arrived at the field where the fair was to be held, Rosalie saw that it was the same field where the old man had given her the picture. Not many caravans had arrived, for Thomas had come very early.

Before Rosalie said goodbye, she whispered a few words in the old woman's ear.

The woman answered, "Yes, lass, this very night I will," and gave Rosalie a kiss on her forehead.

Then Rosalie went down the caravan steps. The Good Shepherd who had helped her as far as this would never leave her now—this was her one comfort. Yet she could not help feeling very lonely as she went down the streets and peeped in at the windows as she passed by.

In nearly every house a bright fire was burning, and tea was ready on the table. In some, families were just sitting down to their evening meal; in all, there was an air of comfort and rest.

Rosalie was out in the cold, muddy, damp streets alone— out in the darkness and the rain, and only five miles from her Aunt Lucy's house!

She sighed deeply as she thought of going alone down those lonely country roads, without a light, and without a friend to take care of her. Yet she was even more afraid to wander alone about the streets of Pendleton.

Even now there were very few people about. She must find someone at once to show her the way to Melton.

She passed a small row of houses built close to the street. Most of them were shut up for the night, but through the cracks of the shutters Rosalie could see the bright lights within.

But the last house in the row was not yet shut up, and as

Rosalie came near to it she saw a small figure come out of the door and go up to the shutters to close them. The fasteners which were on the shutters had caught in the hook on the wall, and the little girl was too short to unloose it. She was standing on tiptoe, trying to undo it, when Rosalie came up.

"Let me help you," she said, running up and unfastening the shutter.

"I'm extremely obliged to you," said a voice behind her, which made Rosalie start.

It was no child's voice; it was a voice she knew well, a voice she had often longed to hear. It was Mother Manikin's voice!

With a cry of joy, Rosalie flung herself into the little woman's arms.

Mother Manikin drew back at first. It was dark, and she could not see Rosalie's face.

So Rosalie said, in a tone of distress, "Mother Manikin, dear Mother Manikin, don't you know me? I'm Rosalie Joyce."

The little, old woman was full of love and sympathy in a moment. She dragged Rosalie into a warm kitchen at the back of the house, where the table was spread for tea, and a kettle was singing cheerily on the fire. She sat on a stool with both her small hands grasping Rosalie's.

"And now, child," she said, "how did you ever find me?"

"I didn't, Mother Manikin," said Rosalie. "We found each other!"

"What do you mean?" said the old woman.

"Why, Mother Manikin, I didn't know you were here. I didn't know who it was till I had finished unfastening the shutter!"

Mother Manikin's Chairs

"Bless me, child, then what brings you out at this time of night? Has your caravan just arrived at the fair?"

"No, Mother Manikin, I've not come to the fair. I'm alone, and I have five miles further to walk."

"Tell me all about it," said Mother Manikin.

So Rosalie told her all—told her how and where her mother had died; told her about the lodging house, and the lady of the house; told her about her father's marriage and death; told her of her Aunt Lucy, and the letter and the locket; told her everything, as she would have told her own mother. Mother Manikin had a motherly heart, and Rosalie knew it; and the tired girl felt a wonderful sense of comfort and peace through pouring out her sorrows into those sympathetic ears.

But the little woman suddenly jumped up, saying hurriedly, "Wait a minute, child. Here's a strange kitten got in."

She was just going to shoo out the little black stranger, which was mewing loudly under the table, when Rosalie stopped her.

"Please, Mother Manikin, that's my kitten. She has come with me all the way, and she's very hungry. That's why she makes such a noise."

In another minute, a saucer of milk was placed on the rug before the fire, and the kitten had enough and to spare.

Rosalie was very grateful to Mother Manikin, and very glad to be with her. Just as she was finishing her story the large clock in the corner of the kitchen struck seven, and Rosalie jumped to her feet.

"Mother Manikin," she said. "I must be off. I've five miles further to walk."

"Stuff and nonsense!" said the old woman. "Do you think

181

I'm going to let you go tonight? Not a bit of it, I can tell you! Old age must have its liberties, my dear, and I'm not going to allow it."

"Oh, Mother Manikin," said Rosalie. "What do you mean?"

"What do I mean, child? Why, that you're to sleep here tonight and then go to your aunt's tomorrow, all rested and refreshed. That's what I mean. Why, I have ever such a nice house here, bless you," said the little woman. "Just you come and look."

She took Rosalie upstairs, and showed her the neat bedroom in the front of the house, and another room over the kitchen, which Mother Manikin called her greenhouse (for in it, arranged on boxes near the window, were all manner of flowerpots containing flowers, ferns, and mosses).

"It's a nice sunny room, my dear," said Mother Manikin, "and it's my hobby, you see. These little plants are my hobby. I live here alone, and they're company, you see. And now come downstairs and see my parlor."

The parlor was in the front of the house, and it was the shutters of this room which Mother Manikin had been closing as Rosalie came up. A bright lamp hung from the ceiling of the room, and white muslin curtains adorned the window. But what struck Rosalie most of all was that the parlor was full of chairs. There were rows of chairs; indeed, the parlor was so full of them that Mother Manikin and Rosalie could hardly find a place to stand.

"What a number of chairs you have here, Mother Manikin!" said Rosalie in amazement.

The old woman laughed at the astonished look on her face.

"Rosalie, child," she said. "Do you remember how you talked to me that night when we sat up in the caravan? Do you remember how I looked at your picture, and you told me all about it?"

"Yes, Mother Manikin," said Rosalie. "Of course I can remember that."

"And do you remember a *question* that you asked me then, Rosalie? 'Mother Manikin,' you said, 'has He found *you?*' And I thought about it for a long time, and then I told you the truth. I said, 'No, He hasn't found me.' But if you asked me that question tonight, Rosalie, if you asked 'Do you think the Good Shepherd has found you *now*, Mother Manikin?' I should tell you, Rosalie, that He went about to seek and save them which were lost, and that one day, when He was seeking, He found little Mother Manikin!

"I cried out to Him that I was lost and wanted finding, and He heard me. He heard me, and He carried me on His shoulders, rejoicing!"

Rosalie could not help crying when she heard this, but her tears were tears of joy.

"So I gave up the fairs, child," Mother Manikin continued. "I told them old age must have its liberties, and I brought away my savings, and a little sum of money I had of my own, and I took this house. So that's how it is," said the little, old woman.

"But the chairs?" asked Rosalie.

"Yes, the chairs," repeated the old woman. "I'm coming to that now. I was sitting one night thinking, my dear, over the kitchen fire. I was thinking about the Good Shepherd, and how He had died for me, just so that I might be found and brought back to the fold. And I thought, child, when He had been so good to me, it was very bad of me to do nothing

183

for Him in return, nothing to show Him I'm grateful, you see. I shook my fist, and I said to myself, 'You ought to be ashamed of yourself, Mother Manikin, you ungrateful, old thing!'

"But then, Rosalie, I began to think, 'What can I do?' I'm so little, you see, and many folks laugh at me and run after me when I go out.

"There seemed nothing for me to do for the Good Shepherd. So I knelt down, child, and I asked Him, 'Good Shepherd, have you got any work for a woman only three feet high? Because I do love you, and want to do your will.'

"Well, Rosalie, child, it came quite quick after that. Mr. Westerdale called and said, 'Mother Manikin, I want to have a Bible meeting for some of the women round here. There are mothers who have babies, and can't get to any place of worship, and a few more who are often ill and can't walk far. Do you know anybody in this road who would let me have a room for my class?'

"Well, child, I danced for joy. I really did, child. I danced like I hadn't danced since I left the Royal Show. So Mr. Westerdale, he says, 'What's the matter, Mother Manikin?' He thought I'd gone clean off my head!

" 'Why, Mr. Westerdale,' I cried, 'there's something I can do for the Good Shepherd, even though I'm only three feet high!'

"So then he understood, and he finds my parlor very convenient, and the people come every week. Tonight is always a happy night for me.

"So that's what the chairs are for. Mr. Westerdale will be here in a minute. He always takes a cup of tea with me before the folks come."

She had no sooner said the words than a rap was heard at

the door, and the little woman hurried to open it for Mr. Westerdale. He was an old man, with a rosy, good-tempered face, and a kind and cheerful voice.

"Well, Mother Manikin," he said, as he came into the kitchen, "you have a good cup of tea ready for me, as usual! What a good, kind woman you are!"

"This is a young friend of mine, Mr. Westerdale," said Mother Manikin, introducing Rosalie.

But Rosalie needed no introduction. She shook hands with the old man, and then darted out of the room and, in another minute, returned with her bag, which she had left upstairs. Hastily undoing it, she took from it her picture—the picture through which God had done so much for her and her mother and Mother Manikin.

Holding it up before the old man, she cried out, "Please, sir, it's quite safe. I've kept it all this time, and I do love it so!"

For Mr. Westerdale was Rosalie's old friend, who had come to see her in the fair just a year ago. He did not remember her, but he remembered the picture. When Rosalie told him where she had seen him, a recollection of the sick woman and her daughter came back to him. As they sat over their tea, Rosalie told how that picture had been the messenger of God's love. The old man's face became brighter than ever.

Soon after tea the people began to arrive. It was a pleasant sight to see how Mother Manikin welcomed them, one by one, as they came in. They all seemed to know her well, and to love her, and trust her. She had so many questions to ask them, and they had so much to tell her. There was Freddy's cough to be inquired after, and grandfather's rheumatism, and the baby's chickenpox. And

Mother Manikin must be told how Sam had gotten the work he was trying for, and how old Mrs. James had gotten a letter from her daughter at last, and how Mrs. Price's daughter had broken her leg. And Mrs. Price had told them to say how glad she would be if Mother Manikin could go in to see her for a few minutes sometimes.

Mother Manikin had a wonderful way of listening, and *their* troubles were *her* troubles, *their* joys *her* joys.

At last, everyone had arrived, and the chairs in the parlor were filled. The clock struck eight, and they were all still as Mr. Westerdale gave out the hymn. And when the hymn and the prayer were ended, Mr. Westerdale began to speak. Rosalie was sitting close to Mother Manikin, and she listened very attentively to all that the old man said.

The text was, "Though your sins be as scarlet, they shall be as white as snow."

Mr. Westerdale explained that the *scarlet* in the text was used as a *symbol*—or picture—of sin. He said, "God says your sins are as scarlet. No scarlet can enter Heaven. Nothing short of perfect, pure white—or holiness—can admit you or me into Heaven. When we stand before the gate, it will be no use to plead, 'I'm *almost* white,' or 'I'm *nearly* white,' or 'I'm whiter than my neighbors!' Only pure white—holiness as white as snow—will be accepted. One single scarlet spot is enough to shut the gates of Heaven against us forever.

"But God is very forgiving, and if we accept the free gift which He has offered us our scarlet sins will become as white as snow! Dear friends, *this* is the way to gain entrance into Heaven. The gift is the Lord Jesus Christ, who has been punished instead of us, and who has taken all our sins upon himself just as if they were His own sins. He has been punished for those sins as if He had really done wrong. The sins had to be punished, but Jesus took the punishment so we would not have to!

"The great God who loves us planned all this. And now He can forgive us our sins because the punishment is over. Not only can He forgive but He can also forget. He can blot out our sins and make us clean and white—as white as snow!

"This, then, is the offer Jesus makes to you tonight. 'Come now,' He cries, 'only accept My offer.' Only take the Lord Jesus Christ as your Savior; only ask Him to wash you in His blood; only see, by faith, that He died in your place *instead* of you. And your sins—your scarlet sins—shall be made as white as snow.

"This very night, before you lie down to sleep, you can be made so white that you can stand before God without shame or fear. So white, that you will be fit to stand amongst that great multitude which no man can number, who have washed their robes and made them white in the blood of the Lamb. The Good Shepherd wants you to call out to Him now."

CHAPTER 21

In Sight of Home

WHEN the service was over, the people left. Mr. Westerdale, Mother Manikin and Rosalie sat together near the fire, talking. The old man was encouraged by all that he heard from Rosalie. He had sometimes wondered whether his visits to the fair had done the slightest good to anyone. Now that he heard how God had blessed this one picture, he felt strengthened and cheered.

Next Sunday was the Sunday for him to visit the shows, he said, and he would go there this year with more hope and more faith than ever before! He explained that he believed he would not only be working *for* God, but would be working *with* God.

"There is a great difference between the two," he said, thoughtfully. "I think, perhaps, I did not realize it until last night!"

When Rosalie heard this she begged him to be sure to see the woman with whom she had traveled. She told him to look out for the caravan over the door of which was written, "Lord Fatimore and other Pleasing Varieties," for there, she felt certain, he would find a work to do. And she did not forget to ask him to inquire for Jinx, and to speak to him also.

When Mr. Westerdale had said goodnight and was gone away, Mother Manikin insisted that Rosalie go to bed at once, for the girl was very weary after her long and tiring day.

Rosalie slept soundly, and in the morning awoke to find Mother Manikin standing beside her with a cup of tea in her hands.

"Come, child," she said, "drink this before you get up."

"Oh, Mother Manikin," said Rosalie, sitting up. "How good you are to me!"

"Bless you, child," said the old woman. "I only wish you could stay with me always. Now, child, if you find when you get to Melton that it isn't convenient for you to stay with your Aunt Lucy, you just come back to me. Dear me, how comfortable you and I could be together! I'm lonesome at times here, and want a bit of company. My little bit of money is enough for both of us. So, if you don't find all quite straight at Melton—if you think it puts them out to take you in—you come to me. Now I've said it, and when I've said it I mean it. Old age must have its liberties, and I must be obeyed!"

"Dear Mother Manikin!" said Rosalie, putting her arms round the old woman's neck, "I can never, never, never say thank you often enough!"

After breakfast Rosalie continued with her journey, with the black kitten sitting in her arms. Mother Manikin insisted on wrapping up a little parcel, containing lunch for Rosalie to eat on her way.

As she stood on the doorstep to see Rosalie off, she called out after her, "Now child, if all isn't convenient, come back here tonight. I shall be looking out for you."

Rosalie waved goodbye and started off quickly. She reached the field where the fair was to be held. What memories it brought to her mind of when she had arrived there in the caravan with her sick mother. It had been just one year ago.

Not many shows had reached the place yet, for it was three days before the fair would begin. In one corner of the field Rosalie discovered the bright yellow caravans of the show of "Lord Fatimore and other Pleasing Varieties." She could not pass by without going to the caravan to thank Old Mother, Thomas and Jinx for their kindness to her the day before.

Mother was having a great wash of all Thomas's clothes—as well as those of Lord Fatimore, and Jinx, and her own. She was standing at the door of the caravan washing, and Jinx was busily engaged hanging the clothes out on a line which had been stretched between the two caravans.

"Halloa, young 'un!" called Jinx, as Rosalie came up. "And where have *you* sprung from?"

Rosalie told him she had just spent the night with a friend who lived in the town, and was going to continue her journey.

"Young 'un," said Jinx. "I haven't forgot what you told me about that there picture."

But he would say no more.

Then Rosalie went up to the woman, who did not see her till she was close to the caravan steps. The woman was hard at work at her washing, with Skirrywinks sitting on her shoulder, and Spanco—the pigeon—on her head.

"Oh, it's you!" she said to Rosalie. "I *am* glad to see you again. I was thinking about you just now."

"Were you?" said Rosalie, sounding surprised. "What were you thinking?"

"I was thinking over what we talked about yesterday— about the lost sheep."

"Did you ask the Good Shepherd to find you?" asked Rosalie.

"Oh yes!" said the woman. "But instead of the Good Shepherd finding me, I think I'm further away from the fold than ever. Leastways, I never knew I was so bad before!"

"Then the Good Shepherd is going to find you," said Rosalie. "He waits until we know we are lost, and then He is ready to find us at once!"

"Oh! I do hope so," said the woman. "You'll think of me sometimes, won't you?"

"Yes, I'll never forget you," promised Rosalie.

"Will you come in and rest a bit?"

"No, thank you," said Rosalie. "I must go now. I wanted to say goodbye to you, and to thank you for being so kind to me yesterday."

"Bless you!" said the woman, heartily. "It was nothing to speak of. Goodbye, child, and mind you think of me sometimes."

So Rosalie left the fair-field and turned on to the road to Melton. What a strange feeling came over her then. She was within five miles of her Aunt Lucy, and was really going to her at last! She longed to see that face which she had gazed at so often in the locket! She longed to deliver her mother's letter, and to see her Aunt Lucy reading it! Often—very often—all this had been on her mind by day, and had mingled with her dreams at night!

Yet now that she was really on the road which led up to her Aunt Lucy's door, Rosalie's heart failed her. She looked down at her dress, and saw how very old it was. She took off her hat. The piece of black ribbon which Toby had given her had never before seemed so faded and brown.

What a shabby girl her Aunt Lucy would see coming in at the garden gate! Her thoughts traveled back to the girl she had seen in that garden a year ago—her Aunt Lucy's own little girl. How differently *she* was dressed! How different in every way she was than Rosalie! What if her Aunt Lucy was cross with her for coming? Her father had made a nuisance of himself by writing letters begging for money. Was it likely her aunt would welcome his child?

These were times when Rosalie felt inclined to go back to old Mother Manikin. But she remembered how her mother had said, "If ever you can, dear, you must go to your Aunt Lucy, and give her that letter."

And now, whatever it cost her, Rosalie determined she would go. But she grew more and more unsure as she drew near the village, and walked far more slowly than she had done when she first left the town.

At last the village of Melton came in sight. It was a fine, spring morning, and the sunlight was falling softly on the cottages, the farmhouses, and the beautiful green trees and hedges.

Rosalie rested on a stile before she went further, and the black kitten basked in the sunshine. The nearby field was full of sheep, and Rosalie sat and watched them. It was a large field. There were groups of trees, under the shadow of which the sheep could lie and rest. There was a quiet stream trickling through the field, where the sheep could drink the cool, refreshing water.

As Rosalie watched the sheep, a verse of the psalm which Popsey's old grandfather had read came into her mind: "He maketh me to lie down in green pastures; He leadeth me beside the still waters."

What if the Good Shepherd were about to take her to a green pasture—a quiet, restful home where she could learn more of the Good Shepherd's love? How Rosalie prayed that it might be so! A pleasant rest was what she needed now. She summoned courage and continued on.

It was about twelve o'clock when Rosalie reached Melton. Most of the country people were having their dinner, and few people were in the village street. With a beating heart, Rosalie kept going.

Soon she came in sight of the cottage, in front of which the caravan had stood when she and her mother were there a year ago. There was the cottage, looking just the same as it had then. There was the garden just as before, with the same kind of flowers growing in it; there were the cabbage roses, the southernwood, the rosemary, the sweetbriar, and the lavendar.

The wind was blowing softly, and wafting their sweet fragrance to Rosalie just as it had done a year ago. And there was Rosalie, standing and peeping through the gate, just as she had done then. The woman and her little girl would no doubt be inside somewhere, having their dinner. It seemed to Rosalie like a dream which she had dreamt before. As she looked, tears came in her eyes and fell upon her dusty clothes. She wiped them away, and went on through the village street.

At length she arrived at the vicarage near the church which her mother had longed so much to see. With an unsteady hand she opened the iron gate and walked up the broad gravel path.

There was a large knocker in the middle of the door, with a bell on one side of it. Rosalie did not know whether to knock or to ring, so she stood still without doing either, hoping that someone would see her from the window and come to ask what she wanted.

But as the minutes passed by and no one came Rosalie ventured, very gently and timidly, to rap with the knocker. No one inside the house heard the sound of the knocking. So Rosalie gathered courage and pulled the bell, which rang so loudly that it made her more afraid than ever.

She heard a rustling in the hall and the sound of a quick footstep, and the door was opened. A girl stood before her, dressed in a pretty print dress and white apron, with a neat round cap on her head. Rosalie was trembling so much now that she kept her eyes on the ground and did not speak.

"What do you want, dear?" asked the girl, kindly.

"If you please," said Rosalie, "is Mrs. Leslie in? I have a letter that I want very much to give her."

"No, dear; she's not in just now," said the girl. "Will you leave the letter with me?"

"Oh, please," said Rosalie. "I would very much like to give it to her myself, if you will be so kind as to let me wait till she comes."

"She won't be very long," said the girl. "Sit in the summer house till she returns. It's very pleasant there."

"Oh, thank you," said Rosalie, gratefully.

"I'll show you where it is," said the girl. "It's behind these trees."

As Rosalie was walking to the summer house she ventured for the first time to look into the girl's face. The voice seemed familiar to her, and when she saw the face, the large, brown eyes, the dark hair, and the rosy cheeks, she felt sure she was meeting an old friend.

"Oh, please," she said, stopping suddenly short in the path, "please, aren't you Britannia?"

"How do you know anything about Britannia?" the girl inquired, hurriedly.

"I didn't mean to say Britannia," said Rosalie. "I know you don't ever want to be called *that* again; but, please, you *are* Jessie, are you not?"

"Yes," said the girl. "My name *is* Jessie. But how do you know me?"

"Don't you remember *me?*" asked Rosalie. "We talked in the caravan that windy night, when my mother was so ill."

"Oh, Rosalie!" said Jessie. "Why, to think I never knew you! Why, I shouldn't ever have been here if it hadn't been for you and your mother! Oh, I am glad to see you again! Where are you going to, dear? Is your caravan at Pendleton fair?"

"No, Jessie," said Rosalie. "I don't live in a caravan now. And I've walked here to give a letter from my mother to Mrs. Leslie."

"Then your mother got better after all," said Jessie. "I am so glad. She was so *very* ill that night."

"Oh, no! no! no!" cried Rosalie, with a flood of tears. "No! She didn't get better."

"Poor Rosalie!" said Jessie, putting her arms round her, and shedding tears also. "I am so very, very sorry!"

"Please, Jessie," said Rosalie through her tears. "Did you remember to give Mrs. Leslie my mother's message?"

"Yes, dear, I did. Do you think I would forget anything she asked me? Why, I should never have been here if it hadn't been for your mother."

"Can you remember what you said to Mrs. Leslie, Jessie?"

"Yes, dear. It was the first time she came to our house after I came back. I told her all about what I had done, and where I had been. And then I told her how I had met with a woman who used to know her many years ago, but who hadn't seen her for a long, long time, and that this woman had sent her a message. So she asked me who this woman was and what the message was which she had sent her. I told her that the woman's name was Norah, but I didn't know her other name, and that Norah sent her respects and her love, and I was to say that she had not very long to live, but that the Good Shepherd had sought her and found her and she was not afraid to die. And then, Rosalie, she cried when I told her that. Then she asked me so many questions about your mother, and I told her all I could. I told her how ill she was, and all about you, and how good you were to your mother. And then I told her how your mother talked to me about the Good Shepherd, and how she begged me to ask the Good Shepherd to find me, and how I had done exactly as she begged me, and He was now carrying me in His arms.

"She wanted to know if I could tell her what town would be the next you would stop at, but I couldn't. Now I must go in, dear, and get dinner ready. But I'll tell my mistress as soon as she comes."

So Rosalie sat down in the summer house to wait. But she could hardly sit still a minute, she felt so excited and restless.

CHAPTER 22

Found

HE time that Rosalie waited seemed very, very long to her. Every minute was like an hour, and at the least sound she jumped from her seat and looked down the gravel path. But it was only a bird, or a falling leaf, or some other slight sound, which Rosalie's anxious ears had exaggerated.

At last, when the sound she had been listening for so long really did come, when footsteps were heard on the gravel path, Rosalie sat very still. In a moment, all the fears she had had by the way returned.

They were very quick and eager footsteps which Rosalie heard. Suddenly her Aunt Lucy entered the summer house and Rosalie found herself locked in her arms.

"Oh, Rosalie!" she said, with a glad cry. "Have I really

found you at last?"

Jessie had already told Mrs. Leslie that it was Norah's daughter who was waiting to see her. Rosalie could not speak. For a long time after that she was too full of feeling for any words. And her Aunt Lucy could only say, over and over again, "My dear Rosalie, have I really found you at last?"

It seemed to Rosalie like the Good Shepherd speaking to His lost sheep, more than anything she had ever heard before.

"Have you been looking for me, Aunt Lucy?" she said at last.

"Yes, darling, indeed I have!" said her aunt. "Ever since Jessie came with the message, I have been trying to find out where you were. But I lost all clue to you, and was almost giving up in despair. I've found you now, darling, and I am so very thankful!"

Rosalie opened her bag and took out the precious letter. Her Aunt Lucy's hand trembled as she opened it. Then she began to read, but her eyes were so full of tears that she could hardly see the words:

MY OWN DEAR SISTER,

I am writing this letter with the faint hope that Rosalie may one day give it to you. It ought not to be a faint hope, because I have turned it so often into a prayer. Oh, how many times I have thought of you since we last met, how often in my dreams you have come to me and spoken to me!

I am too ill and too weak to write much, but I want to tell you that your many prayers for me have been answered at last. The lost sheep has been found, and has been carried back to the fold. I think I must be the greatest sinner who ever lived, yet I believe my sins are washed away by the blood of Jesus.

I know I do not deserve any favor from you, and you cannot think what pain it gives me to think how often you have been asked for money in my name! That has been one of the greatest trials of my unhappy life.

But if you can care for my Rosalie, oh, dear sister, I think even in Heaven I shall know it. I would ask you to do it, not for my sake, for I deserve nothing but shame and disgrace, but for the sake of Him who has said, "Whoso shall receive one such little child in my name receiveth me."

Your Loving Sister
NORAH

"When did your mother write the letter, Rosalie?" Aunt Lucy asked.

Rosalie told her that it was written only a few days before her mother died. Then she put her hand inside her dress and brought out the locket, which she laid in Mrs. Leslie's hand.

"Do you remember *that*, Aunt Lucy?" she said.

"Yes, darling, I do," said her aunt. "I gave that to your mother years ago, before she left home. I remember I saved up my money for a very long time so I could buy it."

"My mother loved that locket so much," said Rosalie. "She said she had promised you she would keep it as long as she lived; and I was to tell you she had kept her promise, and had hidden it away, lest anyone should take it from her. I have tried so hard to keep it safe since she died; but we have been in a great big lodging house all the winter, and I was so afraid it would be found and taken from me."

"Where is your father?" asked Aunt Lucy.

"He's dead," said Rosalie. "He has been dead more than a week." And she told of the accident, and the death in the hospital.

"Then you are *my* girl now, Rosalie," said her Aunt Lucy. "My own girl, and no one can take you from me."

"Oh, Aunt Lucy, may I *really* stay?"

Found

"Why, Rosalie, I have been looking for you everywhere, and my only fear was that your father would not want to part with you. But now, before we talk anymore, you must come in and see your uncle. He is very anxious to see you."

Rosalie felt rather afraid again when her aunt said this. But she rose up to follow her into the house. Then she remembered her kitten, which she covered with her shawl, in a corner of the summer house.

"Please, Aunt Lucy," said Rosalie. "Is there a bird?"

"Where, dear?" said Mrs. Leslie, looking round her. "I don't see one."

"No, not here in the garden," explained Rosalie. "I mean, in your house. Do you have one in a cage?"

"No, there's no bird. What made you think there was one?"

"Oh, I'm so glad, so very, very glad!" said Rosalie, with tears in her eyes. "Then may I bring her?"

"Bring who, Rosalie dear? I don't understand."

"Oh, Aunt Lucy, don't be angry. I have a little kitten here, under my shawl. We love each other so much, and if she had to go away from me I think she would die. She loved me when no one else in the lodging house did, except Betsey Ann; and if only she may come I'll never let her go in any of the best rooms, and I won't let her be any trouble." When she had said this she lifted up the shawl, and brought out the black kitten, which looked up into Aunt Lucy's face.

"What a dear kitten!" said Aunt Lucy. "May *will* be pleased with it. She is so fond of kittens, and only the other day I promised her I would get one. Bring her in, and she shall have some milk."

A great load was lifted off Rosalie's heart when her Aunt Lucy said this.

Found

Rosalie's uncle, the minister of the village church, received her very kindly, and said, with a pleasant smile, that he was glad the little prairie flower had been found at last, and was to blossom in his garden. Then Rosalie went upstairs with her Aunt Lucy to get ready for dinner. She thought she had never seen such a beautiful room as her aunt's bedroom. The windows looked out over the fields and trees to the blue hills beyond.

Then her aunt went to a wardrobe which stood at one end of the room, and brought out a parcel, which she opened, and inside Rosalie saw a beautiful, black velvet dress.

"This is a dress which I bought for my daughter, May," said her aunt. "But I think it will fit you. Try it on."

"Oh, Aunt Lucy!" said Rosalie. "What a beautiful dress! But won't my cousin May want it?"

"No. May is away," said Mrs. Leslie. "She is staying with your Uncle Gerald. There will be plenty of time to have another dress made for her before she returns. Did your mother tell you of our brother Gerald?"

Rosalie said that she had, but that her mother had not been able to see him.

"He's very different now," said Aunt Lucy. "I am sure he will want to meet his sister's daughter!"

Rosalie hardly knew herself in the new dress, and she felt very shy at first. But it fit her perfectly, and her aunt was very pleased.

Then Aunt Lucy brought a black ribbon, and tied the precious locket round Rosalie's neck. There was no longer any need to hide it.

That afternoon Rosalie and her Aunt Lucy had a long talk. Rosalie gave her aunt the story of her life, going back as far as she could remember. Mrs. Leslie listened eagerly to anything about her sister. She asked many questions and hid many tears.

When Rosalie had finished, her aunt told her once more how glad and thankful she was to have her there. Rosalie slipped her hand in that of her Aunt Lucy when she said this.

"So now, Rosalie, you must look upon me as your mother," said Mrs. Leslie. "You must tell me all your troubles, and ask me anything you want, just as you would have asked your own mother."

"Please, Aunt Lucy," said Rosalie, gratefully, "I think the pasture is very green indeed."

"Tell me what you mean," said her aunt.

"I mean, Aunt Lucy, I have been very lonely and often very miserable lately. But the Good Shepherd has brought me at last to a very green pasture. Don't you think He has?"

But Mrs. Leslie could only answer Rosalie by taking her in her arms and holding her tight. Just like the Good Shepherd! thought Rosalie.

That night, when Rosalie went upstairs to bed, Jessie came into her room to bring some hot water.

"Oh, Jessie," said Rosalie, "how are Maggie and the baby?"

"To think you remembered about them!" said Jessie. "They are both well. Oh, you must see them soon."

"Then they were all right when you got home?" asked Rosalie, anxiously. "Were they, Jessie?"

"Oh yes, God be thanked!" said Jessie. "I didn't deserve it. Oh, how often I thought of those children when I lay awake those miserable nights in the circus. They had cried themselves to sleep, poor things. When my mother came back she found them lying asleep on the floor."

"Wasn't she very worried?" asked Rosalie.

"Yes, she was," said Jessie.

"What did she say when you came back?"

"Oh! she wasn't angry a bit," said Jessie. "Only she cried so, and was so glad to have me back that it seemed almost worse to bear than if she had scolded!"

"Is everything all right now?" asked Rosalie.

Jessie smiled. "God has been good to all of us. Mrs. Leslie said I could come here and be her housemaid. My mother says it's a grand thing to lie down to sleep at night feeling that her children are all safe; and she can never thank God enough for all He has done for me. I told her about you and your mother, and she prays for you every day so that God may bless you. Only I didn't know that your mother and Mrs. Leslie were *sisters*. I thought they had just been friends."

The next morning, when Rosalie opened her eyes, she could not at first remember where she was. She had been dreaming that she was in the dismal lodging house, and that Betsey Ann was touching her hand and waking her for their ten minutes' reading.

But when she looked up, it was only her black kitten, which was feeling strange in its new home, and had crept up to her, and was licking her arm.

"Poor little kitten!" said Rosalie, as she stroked it gently. "You don't know where you are." The kitten purred contentedly when its mistress comforted it, and Rosalie began to look round the room.

It was her Cousin May's room, and her Aunt Lucy said she could sleep there until another room just like it was made ready for her. Rosalie was lying in a small, iron bedstead with white muslin hangings. She peeped out of her little nest into the room beyond.

Found

Through the window she could see the fields and the trees and the blue hills, just as she had done from her Aunt Lucy's windows. The furniture of the room was small and very neat. Rosalie looked at it with admiring eyes. Over the wash stand, and over the chest of drawers, and over the table were hung beautiful, illuminated texts, and Rosalie read them one by one as she lay in bed. There was also a bookcase full of May's books, and a wardrobe for May's clothes. Rosalie wondered what her cousin was like, and she wished the time would arrive for her to come home!

Then Rosalie jumped out of bed, and went to the window to look out. The garden beneath her looked very lovely in the bright morning sunshine. The roses and geraniums and jessamine were just in their glory, and underneath the trees she could see patches of ferns and mosses. She wished her mother could have been there to see them also. She had always loved flowers so much.

Rosalie dressed herself, and went out into the garden. She thought how sweet and peaceful everything seemed. Going to the gate—that same gate which she had looked through a year before—Rosalie gazed out into the distance. As she was doing so, she heard the sound of wheels, and three or four caravans bound for Pendleton fair went slowly down the road.

A rush of feeling came over Rosalie as she looked at them! How kind the Good Shepherd had been to her! Here she was, safe and sheltered in this quiet, happy home. Rosalie looked up at the blue sky above, and said from the bottom of her heart, "Good Shepherd, I thank you so very much for bringing me to this green pasture. Help me to love you and please you more than ever. Amen."

CHAPTER 23

The Green Pasture

THAT morning, after breakfast, Mrs. Leslie took Rosalie with her in the pony carriage to Pendleton. She wanted to buy the furniture for the new bedroom.

Rosalie enjoyed the drive, and was delighted with all the purchases which her aunt made.

When they were finished, Rosalie said, "Aunt Lucy, do you think we have time to call for a minute on old Mother Manikin? She will want to hear whether I got safely to Melton."

Mrs. Leslie willingly agreed. She had felt very grateful to the old woman for all her kindness to her sister and her niece, and she was glad of an opportunity to thank her for it.

They found Mother Manikin very poorly, but very pleased indeed to see Rosalie. She had been taken ill in the night, she said, quite suddenly. It was something the matter with her heart. In the morning she had asked one of the neighbors to go for the doctor, and he said it was not right for her to be in the house alone.

"So what am I to do, ma'am?" said Mother Manikin. "Here's the doctor says I must have a maid, but I can't think of where to find one. You couldn't tell me of a girl, could you, ma'am? I can't give very high wages, but she would have a comfortable home."

"Oh! Aunt Lucy," cried Rosalie, springing from her seat, "what do you think of Betsey Ann? Would *she* do?"

"And who's Betsey Ann?" inquired Mother Manikin.

Rosalie told Betsey Ann's story. She told how she had been born in a workhouse, how she had never had anyone to love her, and how she had been scolded and found fault with from morning till night.

"She shall come at once," Mother Manikin said as soon as Rosalie had finished. "Tell me where she lives, and I'll get Mr. Westerdale to write to her."

"Oh, but she can't read," said Rosalie, sounding very alarmed. "Her mistress would *never* let her have the letter if she read it first. What are we to do?"

When Mother Manikin heard where Betsey Ann lived, she said there would be no difficulty at all about it. Mr. Westerdale had a friend there. She often heard him speak of him, and he would be able to go to the house and make it all right.

So Rosalie felt comforted about poor Betsey Ann.

Rosalie's first week passed very happily. She walked and read and talked with her Aunt Lucy, and went with her to see the people in the village, and grew to love her aunt more day by day, and was more and more thankful to the Good

Shepherd for the green pasture to which He had brought her.

After a week cousin May came home. Rosalie liked her as soon as she saw her. But it was no strange face to Rosalie—it was a face she had often gazed at and studied, for May was the image of the girl in the locket. It might have been her own picture, she was so like her mother at that age.

May and Rosalie were friends at once, and from that time on had everything in common. They did school lessons together, they walked together, and they played together.

Sometime after May's return, the girls went together in the pony carriage to Pendleton. They had two important things to do there. One was to buy a present for Popsey, the little girl with the pitcher of milk; and the other was to call on Mother Manikin to see if Betsey Ann had arrived.

The two girls each had a half sovereign given them by Mr. Leslie, and Rosalie intended to spend hers on something for little Popsey. The difficulty was to choose what it should be. All the way to Pendleton, May was suggesting different things—a book, a workbox, a writing case—but at the mention of all these Rosalie shook her head.

"Popsey is too small for any of these," she said. "She cannot read, nor sew, nor write."

So May proposed a doll, and Rosalie thought that was a very good idea.

Palmer, the Leslie's old coachman, was asked to drive to a toy shop. There, after a long consultation, and inspecting many wax dolls, composition dolls, china dolls, rag dolls, and wooden dolls, a beautiful china doll was chosen, and wrapped for Popsey.

But Rosalie still had some money left, so she also chose a spectacle case for Popsey's grandfather, and a little milk jug for the kind, old grandmother. The milk jug was white, and the handle was shaped like a cat climbing up the side of the jug and peeping into the milk. Rosalie was delighted with this as soon as she saw it. She had not forgotten the little pitcher of milk, and she thought that the cat on the milk jug would remind Popsey of the black kitten which she had been so fond of.

All these parcels were carefully put under the seat in the pony carriage, and then they drove to Mother Manikin's.

Who should open the door but Betsey Ann, dressed very neatly in a clean calico dress, and white cap and apron. Betsey Ann's clattery old shoes and her rags and tatters were things of the past. She looked an entirely different girl.

"La, bless you!" she cried when she saw Rosalie. "I'm right glad to see you again." And then she suddenly turned shy, as she looked at the two girls, and led the way to the parlor where Mother Manikin was sitting.

The old lady was full of praises for her new maid, and Betsey Ann smiled from ear to ear with delight.

"Are you happy, Betsey Ann?" whispered Rosalie, as May was talking to Mother Manikin.

"Happy!" exclaimed Betsey Ann, "I should say I am! I never saw such a good little thing as she is. Why, I've been here a whole week, and never had a cross word—I declare I haven't. Did you ever hear the like of that?"

"Oh, I am so glad you are happy!" said Rosalie.

"Yes, He—I mean the Good Shepherd—*has* been good to me," said Betsey Ann. "But wait a minute, Rosalie," she said, as she saw that Rosalie was preparing to go. "I've got a letter for you."

"A letter for me!" exclaimed Rosalie. "Who can it be from?"

"I don't know," said Betsey Ann. "It came the day after you left, and I kept it, in the hope of being able to send it someday. I just happened to be cleaning the doorstep of the lodging house when the postman brought it. Says he, 'Does Miss Rosalie Joyce live here?' So I says, 'All right, sir, give it to me,' and I caught it up quick, and poked it in my pocket. I wasn't going to let *her* get it! I'll fetch it for you if you'll wait a minute."

When Betsey Ann came downstairs, she put the letter in Rosalie's hand. It was in very uneven writing, and Rosalie could not in the least imagine from whom it had come.

DEAR MISS ROSIE,

This letter is to tell you that I can now write. When you helped me to read, I wanted to write as well. Old Mother and Thomas Carter have showed me how. I am sorry if this is not very good writing.

I want you to know that the Good Shepherd has found me. I see now why you were so pleased when He found you.

Perhaps you are not still at the lodging house. Anyway, I hope you gets this letter all right. Maybe I will see you at the fairs one day.

Yours respectfully,
Toby

Rosalie smiled to herself as she read the letter, and folded it up and put it carefully in her pocket. It was a precious letter, and she was so very pleased to hear that Toby was well.

"Mother Manikin," Rosalie said when they were leaving. "Can you get a message to your friends at the Royal Show of the Dwarfs?"

"Of course, my dear," Mother Manikin replied brightly.

"What is the message to say?"

Rosalie explained that she wanted Toby to call in at her uncle and aunt's house next time he was passing to Pendleton fair. She was sure Aunt Lucy would not mind.

"And he can always stop off here and see me if it's convenient for him," Mother Manikin added. "A good lad, is that Toby."

Rosalie did not grow tired of her green pasture as she grew older. She became more and more thankful. Toby called at the vicarage in Melton several times. He was always gladly received by the whole family. Then one year Toby did not come alone—he brought a wife. The two of them stood shyly in the doorway while Rosalie called out in great excitement for May to come.

The next year there was a baby to be introduced. Rosalie picked him up and declared that he was *just* the image of Toby!

"The Good Shepherd has been good to me, Miss Rosie," said Toby, pleased that Rosalie was holding his son. "I shall never forget what you told me about the way He was looking for me. I could understand that He was looking for other people, but I couldn't see that He was looking for *me*. But He was, Miss Rosie, and then he found me. That's what Jesus says in the Bible about the lost sheep. 'He kept looking until He found it.' That's true, that is, Miss Rosie. That's the honest truth!"

"I still have my picture," said Rosalie. "It's in my room. I often look at it and say, 'That's me the Good Shepherd is holding in his arms. Rosalie Joyce—found wandering and brought safely home!' "

"Oh, Miss Rosie," said Toby. "I'm so glad!"

"And I'm glad too," replied Rosalie. "Glad for both of us. Don't forget, Toby, the Good Shepherd has plenty for us to do for Him."

And so ends the story about the lessons learned by Rosalie in her PEEP BEHIND THE SCENES.

Thrills! Action! Suspense! Drama!

Christiana's Journey The vivid account of a young girl's perilous journey. Fraught with unexpected danger, the road she travels is extremely difficult. Illustrates fortitude, perseverance and Christian principles.
P533-4 Trade Paper
ISBN 0-88270-533-4/U.S. Price $4.95

Young Christian's Pilgrimage *Pilgrim's Progress* made alive for young readers. The adventures of young Christian as he battles the dragon-like Appolyon, the Giant Despair, the Wicked Prince and other formidable foes. Children will read this book again and again—right to the last thrilling page!
P534-2 Trade Paper
ISBN 0-88270-534-2/U.S. Price $4.95

Christie's Old Organ A young boy finds life's greatest discovery! This classic story has been a favorite with generations of children. Poignant, charming and captivating!
P532-6 Trade Paper
ISBN 0-88270-532-6/U.S. Price $4.95

Target Earth! John Bunyan's *The Holy War* revised and updated for the 1980s! Follow the adventures of Keerdy and Temar—two angels sent on a mission to earth with a message from God to mankind! But tremendous obstacles stand in their path—will they get through in time?
P536-9
ISBN 0-88270-536-9/U.S. Price $4.95

A Peep Behind the Scenes Mrs. O.F. Walton's touching tale of God's love revealed in hard times and to callous, unloving people.
P538-5
ISBN 0-88270-538-5/U.S. Price $4.95

The Rocky Island and Other Stories Seven classic allegories for children.
P543-1
ISBN 0-88270-543-1/U.S. Price $4.95

**Revised and updated specially for the 1980s
by popular children's author Christopher Wright**

Our exciting new series of Victorian classics for children!

**Bridge Publishing, Inc.
South Plainfield, New Jersey 07080**

Order through your bookstore today!